D1570698

HYPNOTIZING CHICKENS

JULIA WATTS

Bella
BOOKS

2014

Bella Books, Inc.
P.O. Box 10543
Tallahassee, FL 32302

First Bella Books Edition 2014

Editor: Katherine V. Forrest
Cover Designer: Sandy Knowles

ISBN: 978-1-59493-396-7

Other Books by Julia Watts

Bella Books
Wildwood Flowers
Phases of the Moon
Wedding Bell Blues
Finding H.F.
Secret City

Spinsters Ink
Women's Studies
Kind of Girl I Am

Beanpole Books
Kindred Spirits
Free Spirits
Revived Spirits

DISCARD

Acknowledgments

As always, my profound gratitude goes to my wise editor Katherine V. Forrest, to Linda Hill and the Bella Books team, to my family and friends, and to everyone who reads my work.

About the Author

A native of southeastern Kentucky, Julia Watts is the author of numerous books for adults and young adults, including *Secret City*, the Lambda Literary Award finalist *The Kind of Girl I Am*, and the Lambda Literary Award winner *Finding H.F.* She holds an MFA in Writing from Spalding University and teaches at South College and in Murray State University's low-residency MFA program. She lives with her family in Knoxville in a house full of books and pets.

CHAPTER ONE

Forty. Chrys looked around at the students in the classroom and realized she was now twice as old as many of them. Even though forty wasn't approaching the geriatric, it did feel like it should be a mature age—a time by which a gal should have some accomplishments under her belt (she had a few) and a pretty clear vision of where her life was going (she had no idea). There was no arguing that at forty, one was a grownup, and standing in front of a roomful of bored, restless teens and twenty-somethings made her feel like she was looking through the window of a hospital nursery. They were babies. They had just grown up enough to trade their diapers for blue jeans and their pacifiers for cell phones.

Teaching English composition wasn't her preferred way of spending her birthday evening, but Meredith had promised to take her out for a late supper and cocktails once class was over. She let the thought of a dirty martini in a chilled glass fortify her as she turned and wrote the word *Narrative* on the dry-erase board. "Now since you've all had the chance to read Chapter Fourteen—"

"What page is that on?" This was from Brittany in the front row (there were five Brittanys in the class), the blond one who always wore low-cut tops that revealed the tattooed name *Cody* (Husband? Boyfriend? Son?) on her right breast.

"Let me check." Chrys grabbed the textbook off her desk. She had noticed that many students expected her to know page numbers even when she wasn't looking at the textbook, as though being an English teacher meant she was a walking table of contents. "It starts on page two thirty-six," she said, then turned back to the board to write, *A narrative tells a story by relating a sequence of events.*

She turned around from the board to find herself face-to-face with another Brittany, the brown-haired, big-boned one who always seemed to be wearing the same Kenny Chesney T-shirt. "My sister just texted me," Brittany Two said, "and she's watching my baby, but now she has to take her dog to the vet on accounta something he ate." She sounded panicky, but it was the same kind of panicky as when she forgot a pen or a paperclip. Panicky seemed to be her default setting. "If I was to leave now, would I miss anything?"

No, Chrys was tempted to say, we'd halt the class immediately and spend our remaining time praying for your sister's dog's recovery. "Email me, and I'll let you know what you missed," she said instead. "I'm kind of busy lecturing right now."

After Brittany Two's departure, Chrys said, "Now what are some of the elements of narrative—the things we have to have if we're going to write a story?"

"Plot, character, setting, theme," offered Liz from the third row. Liz was in her early thirties, and like many of Chrys's brightest students, was a young mother who had decided to go back to college once her kids reached school age.

"Good," Chrys said, writing the terms on the board. "And of course, a narrative can be fiction or non-fiction—"

Music suddenly blared—the chorus of a pop song celebrating the joys of binge drinking—and it took longer than it probably should have for Chrys to identify it as a ring tone. "Folks," she said, "can we please keep the phones turned off during class?"

Incredibly, the offending party, a jocky-looking guy who owed her two papers, took the call. "Hey," he said, oblivious to all but the person on the other end of the phone. "Not much, just sitting in class."

Six years ago, Chrys had taught a different breed of student at a different breed of school. Conscientious and hard-working, most of them had arrived at college with above-average test scores and a few AP credits. Not all of them were brilliant, of course, but overall they tended to be motivated kids who really flung themselves into the college experience, and working with them Chrys often felt that she learned just as much as she taught.

But then she had gone and done the one thing that always changes everything. She had fallen in love.

Back at Western Carolina State, where Chrys had gotten her first teaching job a decade ago, her work life had been radically different. WCS was in a quaint little town in the mountains. It was a lovely campus with red brick buildings and old trees, and the kids, many of whom came from those mountains with big college dreams, reminded her of herself at their age. The regional university vibe of the school itself was reminiscent of Murray State in Kentucky where Chrys had done her own undergraduate work, so she had felt comfortable there instantly. It didn't hurt that the members of the English department, many of whom were nearing retirement age, treated her like a child prodigy for being a newly minted PhD. When her dissertation on lesbian writers on the Left Bank was published as a book, they threw her a party with cake and ice cream.

Though Chrys had been happy during the work week at the university, she often found herself growing restless on the weekends, so she'd drive to Asheville, the nearest city, to wander the bookstores and funky shops. One Saturday while browsing the lesbian fiction section in Asheville's lesbian-owned-but-not-wholly-lesbian bookstore, she found herself standing beside a tall, athletic-looking blond woman. The woman picked up a copy of Sarah Waters' *Tipping the Velvet*, and Chrys heard herself saying, "That's a fabulous book."

The woman's smile revealed straight white teeth and dimples. "That's what everybody says. I can't believe I haven't read it. They're going to take my lesbian card away."

Chrys wasn't exactly closeted at work, but she wasn't announcing her sexuality from the rooftops either. It was refreshing to hear someone drop being a dyke as an opening conversational gambit. The conversation continued, first over coffee at the bookstore café, then over dinner at a restaurant way out of Chrys's price range that served small mounds of artfully drizzled food on square white plates, then later on the high thread-count sheets in Meredith's room in the Grove Park Inn after sex that was so much better than Chrys's past experiences that it seemed like something else entirely. Chrys was a little shocked at herself for going to bed with a woman on the first date—and an impromptu first date at that. But she had been single for a long time. And she was smitten.

Meredith, it turned out, was a plastic surgeon with a practice at the University of Tennessee Medical Center in Knoxville. Chrys would've ordinarily been turned off by a profession that catered to vanity in an appearance-obsessed culture, but Meredith had explained to her how she had been literally "bitten by" her occupation. As a small child, she had been severely bitten on the face by a neighbor's dog. She would've been permanently disfigured had it not been for the excellent work of a skilled plastic surgeon. Sure, she said, in her profession there was no shortage of Botox and boob jobs and butt lifts, but there was fulfilling work, too: facial reconstruction for victims of house fires and car crashes, new breasts for cancer survivors. Chrys began to feel that she'd judged a whole profession too harshly.

Fortunately, Chrys hadn't been the only one who'd been smitten. Their conversation continued by phone and email and in person once a month when they'd reconnect in Asheville.

They went on for a year like this before Meredith started talking about them living together.

Of course, there was no way Meredith could give up a successful practice, and so, after six months of agonizing, Chrys decided to give up a job she loved for the woman she loved. She moved to Knoxville.

Chrys had only had one other live-in lover, with whom she'd shared a crappy one-bedroom apartment when she was working on her master's degree at the University of Kentucky. Her living situation with Meredith was a far cry from the student slum days. Meredith owned a four-bedroom faux chateau, complete with an Olympic-sized swimming pool, in an upscale Knoxville subdivision called Whittington Manor (all the frou-frou subdivisions in the area seemed to have "-ington" names). A Guatemalan maid was in charge of cleaning the house, and her husband did the mowing, blowing, and landscaping. It took several months for Chrys to feel like a resident in the house instead of one of the staff.

It took Chrys a full year to find a new job, and she wouldn't have found it without a tip from one of Meredith's acquaintances. A nurse who'd been a colleague of Meredith's had taken a teaching job at Hill College and let Meredith know that one of the English faculty members there was retiring. Thanks to the grapevine, Chrys had found herself a gig teaching five sections of freshman comp (plus tutoring four hours a week in the Writing Center) to students pursuing careers as nurses, paralegals, x-ray technicians, and office managers. Her heady days of teaching English majors were gone, but still, she didn't feel she could complain too much. In the past her love life had always taken a backseat to her academic life; it balanced the scales to shift the weight to the other side…especially for a lover as entrancing as Meredith.

Tonight, as her class's nine thirty end time drew nearer, Chrys felt as restless as her students looked. She put them in groups for a while to discuss an essay they had allegedly read. But when she listened in on the discussions, the topics seemed to be what the students were going to eat or drink when they got out of class, what they had done last weekend, and what they were going to do this weekend. By ten after nine, Chrys decided that there was zero chance of any further education occurring and dismissed class.

She was a little early for her meeting time at the Brasserie (or the "brassiere," as they always called it in private), but when she got there, Meredith was already there, waiting at the door, wearing a tailored suit and silk blouse combination that managed to look both professional and sexy. She kissed Chrys's cheek and said, "I see you survived your class."

"Only a little worse for wear," Chrys said. "Nothing a drink won't fix."

"Well, shall we?" Meredith held open the door.

Once they were inside, the fawning commenced. The maitre d', who was young enough to be a student at the university, said, "Dr. Padgett, what a pleasure to see you this evening! We have your special table ready for you."

One of the things Chrys had to get used to in the early days of their relationship was the constant ass-kissing that came with Meredith being a doctor. At first, probably pettily, Chrys had been a little jealous. After all, she had a doctorate, too, and people didn't fall all over themselves ingratiating themselves with her. But the logic behind the ass-kissing was obvious: M.D.s had way more spending power than PhDs in English. And then, too, if you were on a plane and a message came over the speaker saying, "Is there a doctor on board?" there was no doubt what kind of doctor they were asking for. They sure as hell weren't looking for somebody in first class who could analyze the homoerotic imagery in *The Adventures of Huckleberry Finn.*

Once they were seated at their cozy, white-clothed table, Meredith ordered a bottle of champagne and the mussels appetizer that was Chrys's favorite. After the champagne cork popped, Chrys looked around the dimly lit restaurant with its black and white photos of Parisian life. "This is a far cry from the birthdays of my childhood. It was always hot dogs followed by a cake straight out of a Betty Crocker box."

Meredith smiled. "For me it was usually a party with a bakery cake and a clown making balloon animals or something."

It figured. Chrys had grown up a country girl while Meredith was solidly suburban. "How traumatic."

"Not really." Meredith smiled. "I don't share your fear of clowns."

"Which is lucky." Chrys paused for a sip of champagne. "Because, you know, they can smell fear."

Her entree was a buttery filet of sole surrounded by tender-crisp haricots verts. It was funny to compare these green beans with the ones she'd grown up eating back in Kentucky. Nanny would string the beans in the morning and leave them simmering on the stove for hours with a huge slab of bacon. Both Nanny's beans and the Frenchified version in front of her were delicious, but it was hard to think of them as the same vegetable.

Over the meal, Chrys and Meredith chatted about the usual things—Meredith's high-maintenance and sometimes crazy patients, Chrys's high-maintenance and sometimes crazy students, whether or not the new movie they wanted to see would make it to Knoxville's single art-house cinema this weekend.

When dessert arrived, Chrys closed her eyes to better experience her first spoonful of chocolate mousse. "I could fill a bathtub with this stuff and jump in," she said.

"Order a second if you like," Meredith said. "It's your birthday."

"But then my ass would be so wide I wouldn't fit in a bathtub."

"Oh, I don't know. We've got a pretty big bathtub."

It was true. The tub in the master bath was a huge, oval jacuzzi in which they could both sit comfortably and soak up to their shoulders.

"Listen," Meredith said, "I know you said no gifts, but I did get you a little something."

"But—"

"I promise it's just little." Meredith rummaged through her bag.

The first three years of their relationship Meredith had showered Chrys with expensive jewelry—diamond stud earrings from Tiffany, a string of Mikimoto pearls. She had loved them, of course, but she was really more of a funky art-fair jewelry kind of girl. And besides, all the small gift boxes left at her spot on the dinner table or on her pillow had started to make her feel like a mobster's mistress. "You'd better not have the Hope Diamond in there," Chrys said as Meredith continued to search the compartments in her bag.

"Here it is," she said finally and passed Chrys a flat, square box wrapped in purple tissue paper.

Chrys tore into it. "Oh, the Adele CD! Perfect. Thank you."

"Because I've learned to respect your frugality, I shopped at Target instead of Tiffany."

Chrys reached across the table and squeezed Meredith's hand. "And I couldn't be happier."

Back at the house, tipsy from the champagne, Chrys started shedding components of what she called her "teacher drag" as soon as she got in the door. She stepped out of her flats in the foyer and unbuttoned her blouse as she climbed the curving stairs to the bedroom. Soon she was standing in front of Meredith in nothing but her diamond earrings, string of pearls, and black lace bra and panties. "So give me your professional opinion," she said. "Do I look forty?"

"You look like a goddess," Meredith said. "And goddesses are ageless. Besides, you're not allowed to obsess over your age since I'm a decade older than you."

"You don't look it," Chrys said. It was true. Though Meredith had never indulged in the surgical vanity of her patients, she looked much younger than her age. Her face, with its enviable bone structure and strong jawline, was wrinkle-free except for smile lines, and her body was toned from hours of running and tennis. Sometimes, especially when she was in her shorts and T-shirt, her short blond hair tousled after a run, she could almost pass for a teenaged tomboy.

"You're too kind." Meredith leaned in toward Chrys.

Chrys melted into Meredith's kiss and let herself be pushed back onto the bed. Chrys's other live-in lover—almost twenty years ago—had been an enthusiastic neophyte lesbian. They had rolled all over each other like puppies, joyful but lacking finesse.

No one could accuse Meredith of lacking finesse. Maybe it was the same skill that served her well as a surgeon. Her hands were sure and practiced, and she always knew just where to touch, how much pressure to apply, when to speed up, when to slow down. Tonight, with her body loose from champagne, Chrys felt Meredith slide her panties down, and within seconds she came, with three short gasps punctuated by a bark of laughter. "Happy birthday to me," she said.

Meredith kissed her forehead. "Happy birthday to you."

Chrys sat up on one elbow and ran her fingers through Meredith's short blond hair. "And now it's your turn."

Meredith grinned. "It's not my birthday."

Chrys pressed against her. "That's not what I mean, and you know it."

"I know exactly what you mean, but I'm going to have to take a rain check. It's after midnight, and I have to be up at six. And if you recall, champagne makes *you* frisky, but it makes me sleepy."

Chrys recalled no such thing—in fact, their champagne-fueled New Year's Eve celebrations were downright orgiastic—but she nodded anyway. Tired was tired, after all, and Meredith's job did put her under a lot of physical and mental strain. It had been nice of Meredith to wine her and dine her at the end of a long work day when she was no doubt exhausted.

But somehow as Chrys watched Meredith change into an old pair of sweatpants and a Lady Vols T-shirt, she felt a pinprick of anxiety that threatened to deflate her happy mood.

Now their evening together took on the qualities of something Meredith felt obligated to do—no matter how tired she was and no matter how much tireder a late night was going to make her—because it was Chrys's birthday. She was probably being silly, but she couldn't help but feel that Meredith had been showing her a good time without having a good time herself.

CHAPTER TWO

The game was called Five More Papers. Chrys played it sitting at her desk during her office hours. The game consisted of making a series of deals with herself. If she graded five more papers, then she could log onto Facebook and mess around for ten minutes. After the ten minutes on Facebook, if she graded five more papers, then she could eat a Hershey's kiss. Five more papers after that would earn her one video on YouTube.

It wasn't a very fun game, but it was psychologically necessary. With the influx of papers from her sections of composition, she constantly needed to be grading. And yet if she surveyed the stack of papers on her desk and told herself she had to grade all of them, she would find the nearest office with a window so she could jump out of it. If she deceived herself into a sense of accomplishment after each small stack of five, though, eventually all the papers would get graded.

She had always had a knack for self-deception anyway. Hell, until her senior year of college, she had convinced herself that she was straight.

What surprised her most about being a writing teacher was that while she might have been able to help some of her students become better writers, it seemed to come at the cost of making her a worse one. She had always been a good academic writer, never earning anything other than As on her papers as an undergrad and grad student. When she was in the PhD program at Vanderbilt, she got a couple of papers accepted at conferences, and then later there was the publication of her dissertation by a small university press. But since she spent so much time reading freshman-level writing, she found freshman-level mistakes creeping into her own work—using *their* when she meant *there* or *whose* when she meant *who's*. It was almost as if the freshmen gained their writing ability by draining her of hers. They were grammar succubi.

Today she won the biggest prize in the game of Five More Papers. It came when Chrys timed the end of the last stack of five to coincide with the end of her office hours. Going home was the ultimate reward.

When Chrys pulled her bedraggled old Toyota into the driveway, she was surprised that Meredith's gold Lexus was already there. Meredith didn't usually make it home until six at the earliest.

Meredith was sitting on the couch in the living room. She had changed out of her work clothes and into track shorts and a freebie T-shirt from one of the many marathons she'd run. She wasn't crying, but her eyes were puffy as though she had been.

"What's wrong?" Chrys asked. Her usually dormant Appalachian morbidity kicked in, and she ran a mental catalog of loved ones who could've died. Meredith's grammy was most likely, but it could've been Meredith's Aunt Charlotte, too. "Is somebody sick?"

"Nobody's sick," Meredith said. "I came home early so we could talk."

Any momentary sense of relief evaporated. "Uh…is this a 'we need to talk' kind of talk?"

Meredith stopped short of smiling. "I guess it is."

Fear tightened Chrys's stomach. "Is this a 'you'd better sit down' kind of talk?"

Meredith nodded.

Chrys sank into the nearest chair. "Okay, tell me."

Meredith rubbed her face for a moment, then said, "Okay. Chrys, you're one of the most incredible women I've ever met, and this has nothing to do with anything you've said or done. But the heart follows its own path—"

She couldn't stand it. "Just fucking tell me."

"You're right. Nothing I can say is going to make this easier. I've met someone else. Her name is Audrey, and she's a nurse in a practice that's on the same floor as mine."

The shock that rolled through her was probably silly. Meredith had been involved with another woman when she started dating Chrys. She had left the other woman for Chrys, and now she was leaving Chrys for yet another woman. She shouldn't be shocked, but she was. "Is she younger than I am?"

Meredith shook her head. "That's neither here nor there. She's an intelligent, vivacious—"

"Just humor me and answer the question."

"She's twenty-seven, but—"

"Jesus Christ, Meredith! You could be her mother!"

Meredith's gaze turned icy. "Now that's a low blow."

"It's not a low blow. It's a factual statement. You're twenty-three years older than she is! And while we're dealing with facts here, let's see…you're a cosmetic surgeon, and as you get progressively older, your girlfriends get progressively younger. You're the lesbian Dorian Gray!"

"Look, there's no reason for us to say things we don't mean—"

Hot tears spilled onto Chrys's cheeks. "You think I don't mean this? That I'm not entitled to be pissed off? I gave up a tenure-track university job to come here and teach at the McDonald's of higher education."

Meredith held out her hands as if in supplication. "I know you've made sacrifices, and I'm certainly willing to help you—"

"I don't want your money. I never did." Chrys would be lying if she said she hadn't enjoyed some of the luxuries of life with Meredith—the European summer vacations, the Caribbean winter ones—but she'd always been in it for love, not money, and she got pretty sick of the dykes who looked at her like she was some kind of gold digger. "What I want is for you to tell me this. Last night, did you know you'd be having this conversation with me today?"

Meredith's eyes were wet. "Yes."

"Then why did you wait to tell me?"

"Well, Jesus, I figured there's a hot place in hell for people who break up with their girlfriends on their fortieth birthday."

"But waiting till the day after is okay?" Chrys couldn't sit anymore. She had to get up and pace, to do something to fight off the feeling that she was about to fly into bits. "So you take the old girl out to dinner first, feed her and fuck her for old times' sake."

"Stop it, Chrys."

But she couldn't stop. "Of course you can't let her fuck you back because that would be too intimate, wouldn't it? To open yourself up to her when you know what you're going to do to her the next day."

Meredith got up and put her hands on Chrys's shoulders. "It wasn't like that," she said, her voice breaking. "I never meant—"

"Don't even try," Chrys said, shrugging away from Meredith's touch. "Nothing you can say will be the right thing."

* * *

You couldn't accuse Meredith of poor planning. She had arranged to be out of town all weekend (probably with her nearly jailbait girlfriend) so Chrys could have the time to "process and plan." She figured that in Meredith-speak, *process* meant crying and *plan* meant "figure out where you're going to live and how soon you can get the fuck out of my house."

Right now, four hours after the big showdown, Chrys was processing. Or at least that was what she was doing if processing meant curling in a fetal ball on the guest bed, sobbing and staining the pillows with tears and snot. Her first instinct had been to crawl into her bed, but she couldn't bear to be in the bed she'd shared with Meredith. And so she ended up in one of the gigantic house's three guest bedrooms, fitting since Meredith's treatment of her showed that she'd never been considered more than a guest in this house anyway. And now she was a guest who was being asked to leave.

Eventually the sunlight faded, but Chrys couldn't be bothered to turn on the lamp. The rational side of her knew she should get up and drink a glass of water; this much crying was dehydrating. But she didn't really care enough to move. She imagined herself as a dehydrated corpse forgotten in the guest bedroom while Meredith and the new girl started their life together. It would be lesbian Southern gothic.

When the phone rang, her first delusional thought was that it was Meredith saying it had all been a mistake. But the screen showed Aaron's number. Other than Meredith, there were only three people in the world whose calls Chrys answered no matter what: her mother, her grandmother, and Aaron.

Aaron was the one close friend Chrys had made since moving to Knoxville. There were pleasant acquaintances, mostly couples in Meredith's circle of friends. Now, Chrys supposed, the new girl would be socializing with these women. But Aaron was Chrys's and Chrys's alone.

The first time she met Aaron, she took off all her clothes and let him touch her all over. This was the truth, and it was also the source of a running joke between the two of them. Aaron was a massage therapist at a local spa, and Chrys met him when Meredith had bought her a spa gift certificate she hadn't been sure what to do with. A mud bath seemed disgusting, and a chemical peel sounded painful, so she had settled on a massage. As she waited in her spa-issued fluffy robe, she had wondered if she'd made a mistake in agreeing to strip naked and be touched by a stranger. What if the masseuse was the kind of hyper-masculine straight guy she found off-putting? Or what if it was a sexy dyke who made her all self-conscious and giggly?

Chrys couldn't have been more relieved to see that her massage therapist was a whippet-thin, mocha-complexioned, obviously gay man.

During the massage, Aaron let it slip that he had become a massage therapist once it became clear that his bachelor's degree in theater left him unsuited for any type of stable employment. Chrys had asked him his opinion of Tony Kushner, and soon the two of them were off and running on a fascinating conversation about gay theatre even as Aaron kneaded Chrys's buttocks. When he handed her his card at the end of the session, he said, "I'd be very happy if you'd come back for another massage, but I'd be even happier if you'd call me to have lunch or coffee. I could get fired for saying that to a cute guy client, but I figure I'm safe with you."

"And vice versa," Chrys had said.

Many lunches and gallons of coffee had followed, along with occasional movie dates and "girls' nights out." They had a standing date to attend Club XYZ's Night of a Thousand Dollies, an annual charity fundraiser in which local drag queens donned their best (and sometimes worst) Dolly Parton drag.

Chrys stared at Aaron's number on the screen. She didn't feel like talking, but Aaron was too good a friend to ignore. When she said hello, her voice sounded rusty and nasal.

"Um…I'm calling for Chrys?"

"You got her, you dizzy dame."

"I did? Christ on a rope, honeybun, you sound like shit."

"Well, there's a good reason for it. Meredith dumped me."

"What?"

"Don't make me say it again." But his shocked tone was gratifying.

"I'm sorry. It's just…I run through boyfriends like clean pairs of socks, but you and Meredith have been together—what, five years?"

"Six. And apparently my warranty ran out and I've been traded for a newer model."

"Oh, hon, I'm so sorry. Where are you now?"

"In the guest bedroom in the fetal position."

"Well, grab your toothbrush and some jammies and get your booty over here. You don't need to be hanging around the scene of the crime."

* * *

Aaron's apartment was on the second floor of a ramshackle Victorian house in a neighborhood that had undergone Step One of the gentrification process: the gays had moved in. Chrys climbed the outside staircase which was lined with potted herbs and tomato plants. She wiped her eyes and nose before she knocked, but she knew there was no point in doing anything else to improve her appearance. She was an ugly crier, and she'd been crying for hours.

Aaron opened the door and opened his arms. Chrys fell into his slim but muscular frame and sobbed. He kissed the top her head and crooned "I know, I know" the way her mom used to. "Why don't we at least move to the couch?" he said. "We might as well cry in comfort."

On the purple crushed velvet sofa (Aaron had rescued it from the junkyard and reupholstered it himself), Chrys lay with her head in her friend's lap. Between sobs, she managed to choke out the story of the previous twenty-four hours.

"So let me get this straight," he said, stroking her hair. "She took you out for a fancy dinner with champagne and everything. Did she buy you a present?"

"The Adele CD."

"How thoughtful of her to provide a soundtrack for the breakup. Do you think she meant to be sadistic there?"

She hadn't thought about it until Aaron said so, but every song on the Adele album was about breaking up or trying— often unsuccessfully—to move on after breaking up. Would Meredith have been that intentionally cruel? "You know, I honestly don't think she did. I'd said I wanted the album, and I figure she just picked it up at Target along with the toothpaste and never really thought about it. Plus, you don't want to buy an expensive gift for the girl you're going to dump the next day."

"Well, it does suck to turn forty and to turn single in the same twenty-four-hour period," Aaron said.

"It rates pretty high on the suck-o-meter," Chrys said.

"Let me be a mama for a minute, honeybun. When was the last time you had something to eat or drink?"

"I don't remember. Around one, I guess." It seemed like a decade ago when she'd eaten a cheese and tomato sandwich at her desk while grading papers, thinking it was just an ordinary day.

"Okay, sit up. The first thing we're going to do is get you a big glass of water. Then I prescribe a pizza and half a bottle of red wine."

Chrys and Aaron had shared a pizza and a bottle of wine numerous times on this very couch, but right now she couldn't imagine ingesting food. Her throat and stomach felt like she'd swallowed concrete. "I don't think I can eat anything."

"Oh, that's right," Aaron said. "You're one of those people who stops eating when she's upset. As opposed to me…get me upset and I'll eat a whole box of Little Debbies including the cardboard."

"And not gain an ounce," Chrys said. She always marveled at Aaron's inability to gain weight and wished it was one she shared.

"Listen, I'm going to order the pizza, and then I'm going to pour enough wine down you that you won't be able to resist it when it gets here."

Halfway through their second glass, Chrys said, "You know what the worst part is? I changed my life to be with her, and now that she doesn't want me anymore, I can't change it back."

Aaron squeezed her hand. "Well, maybe you can change it forward."

Chrys surprised herself with a little snort of laughter. "What the hell does that even mean?"

Aaron laughed, too. "I have no idea. I guess I'm being nurturing, and it's making me get all Oprah on your ass."

The wine did relax her enough that she was able to manage a slice of pizza (though she was usually a three-slice kind of girl).

"The first thing you've got to do," Aaron said, helping himself to a fourth slice, "is get out of that mausoleum of a McMansion."

"I know, right?" Chrys let Aaron refill her glass. "But I have to figure out somewhere to go." The idea of apartment hunting in her emotional state was overwhelming, but she also couldn't bear the thought of spending another night in what she was already thinking of as "that house."

"Well, I know we're kind of old to do the roommates thing, but I do have an extra bedroom," Aaron said. "You're welcome to crash here for a month or two while you figure things out."

The kindness of Aaron's offer made the tears start again. "Oh, I couldn't possibly impose on you like that…just moving in here like Blanche DuBois."

"Damn it, I'm Blanche. If we're doing that play, you're stuck being Stella. Really, though, honeybun, it'd be no trouble. And if it makes you feel better you can chip in on rent, groceries, and booze. You can think of this place as your own personal flophouse."

Chrys wiped her tears. "Okay. But just for a little while, okay?"

"Okay. Shall I show you to your room?"

The guest bedroom was small, just big enough for a double bed, a dresser, and a little walking space between them. A poster for a university production of *Fences* in which Aaron had starred hung on the wall. A handmade quilt was on the bed, along with a dozing Celie, Aaron's long-lived calico cat.

"Now Miss Celie thinks of this room as hers," Aaron said, "so she may be a little pissy about sharing her bed at first."

"I'm sure we'll get along fine," Chrys said. She liked cats and had owned one back in North Carolina, a tortoiseshell named Djuna who eventually became "Junie." But Meredith was allergic, and so Chrys had given Junie to a friend who still emailed her pictures from time to time. Chrys added Junie to the growing list of Things She Had Given Up to Be With Meredith.

Chrys changed into the T-shirt and shorts Aaron had loaned her and crawled under the quilt beside Celie. She must have used up her daily allotment of tears because none would come, though she felt no less sad than when she'd been sobbing. Sleep wouldn't come either. She lay there, stroking Celie, wondering if she was destined to stay awake all night feeling this empty ache.

But then there was a soft knock at the door and Aaron whispering, "You want some company?"

"Yes, please."

"Scoot over."

They curled up together like kittens in the same litter, and finally Chrys slept.

CHAPTER THREE

It only took three car trips to move her stuff from the house to Aaron's apartment. The first trip had been to haul her clothes, the next two her books. After she filled her car with the last load—six liquor store boxes full of literature and a couple of shoe boxes of CDs—she took one last walk through the house. She knew it would make her cry, but she had to do it anyway.

She passed through the spacious, butter-yellow kitchen with the granite countertops where she and Meredith had stood, chopping vegetables and laughing. She ran her fingers over the oak table in the dining room where the two of them had shared meals from coq au vin to peanut butter and jelly.

The bedroom was the last stop. It hurt too much to look at the bed where they had not only made love but talked and slept and tended to one another in sickness. She turned away and caught her teary reflection in the mirror. She took off her diamond earrings and set them on the dresser. Meredith would probably tell her to keep them, but what was it Ophelia says to Hamlet? "Rich gifts wax poor when givers prove unkind."

She dropped her house key on the dresser next to the jewelry and walked out of the bedroom, down the stairs, and out the door.

It was exhausting to haul all those book-heavy boxes up the stairs to Aaron's apartment. Once she dragged them all into her room, it wasn't clear what to do with them. Should she go ahead and buy a bookcase or just fashion a hobo-style one by turning the boxes sideways and stacking them? Whatever she was doing, she wasn't doing it now. She flopped on the bed next to Celie, who seemed to be occupying the exact same spot she had this morning. Maybe the cat had the right idea. Sleep was a tempting escape. She closed her eyes, only to have them open at the ringing of her phone. She picked it up to see her mom's number. She had given herself the deadline of Sunday night to tell her mom about the breakup, but it looked like the time was now. She took a deep breath and answered.

"There you are, Chrystal!" Her mom's voice was cheerful. "I tried your other number first, but there wasn't nobody home."

Chrys ignored her mother's double negative. She had gone through an arrogant phase in high school during which she had insisted on correcting her family members' grammar, but it had only led to arguments and tears. "Yeah, well, there's a reason for that."

"Your rich lady friend forget to pay the phone bill?" She laughed at her own joke.

"Actually, my rich lady friend broke up with me." As soon as she said it, she started crying like she hadn't since she was a little girl.

"She did what? Wait—you don't have to answer that, I heard you the first time. I just don't believe it."

"She met somebody else. Younger, naturally."

"Now what is the advantage of being with a woman if she's just gonna run off and act like a man?"

"I don't know. Maybe that she couldn't get me pregnant before she left me?"

Her mom laughed. "You're funny even when you're sad. Well, I reckon you know how I always felt about Meredith. I never thought I could trust her as far as I could sling her."

"Apparently you had better sense about her than I did." Chrys was lying back down now, letting her mother's words comfort her.

"Well, I wasn't blinded by sex," her mom said. "She wasn't my type."

Chrys let herself laugh a little. Her mom's views on Chrys's sexuality were complex. On the one hand, she would've liked for Chrys to be straight because she thought it would be easier for all concerned—easier for Chrys who wouldn't have to fear homophobia, easier for the family who wouldn't have to explain why Chrys had never married or reproduced. On the other hand, Chrys's mom believed that a leopard couldn't change its spots. Some people were just made "that way," and Chrys, apparently, was one of them. And at least as a lesbian, Chrys wouldn't do what her straight brother did—move back to the family homeplace with a too-young wife and a toddler whom, he assumed, "Memaw" would be more than happy to pitch in raising.

Chrys figured that when it came down to it, her sexual orientation was just one item on a long list of things about her that her family found baffling. Her parents lived in a holler off a dirt road in Piney Creek, Kentucky, a "town" which had only three places of business: a sawmill, a miniscule post office and a gas station/mini-mart. Chrys's dad had worked in the sawmill until an accident left him one-armed and disabled, and Chrys's mom worked sewing uniforms at a tiny factory in Morgan, the nearest real town. They lived in a little wooden frame house that had once been white but had turned gray with age, and Chrys's grandmother, called "Nanny" by all, lived in a similar but even smaller house further up the holler. As a young child, Chrys had gone to the six-room Piney Grove Elementary, but when she reached middle school age, she had to wait for the bus that would come before dawn to take her to Morgan, picking up other country kids on the way.

Even as a child, Chrys had known that her future was not in the holler. She had too many interests that couldn't be pursued there. Her parents were supportive but confused. They were glad to have her there but weren't sure where she'd come from. They looked at her like a friendly alien who had descended from a spaceship to live with them. They were proud of her achievements, though, and her mom was always supportive. When Chrys was in fifth grade, she had decided that she wanted to be a Famous Author, and her mom took her to Morgan to get her a library card, making it a point to take her to the library every two weeks.

Years later, when Chrys's dissertation was published, her mom had said, "Well, when you was a little girl, you said you wanted to be a famous author, and now you've gone and done it." This was sweet but also hilarious. The print run had only been five hundred.

Today, as always, Chrys's mom was supportive. Even if she didn't fully understand, she understood enough to know that rejection hurts.

Once Chrys had sobbed out her whole sad story, she realized that she had been behaving with the self-absorption of the recently dumped. "I'm sorry. I haven't even asked how you all are."

"We're all right, I reckon. Today Peyton got the bright idea to try to jump off the porch roof onto the trampoline. Thank the Lord she has good aim. For somebody that calls herself a princess, she's tough as a cob."

Chrys's brother Dustin's desire to name his firstborn after his favorite football player hadn't been dimmed by the fact that she was a girl. Peyton, he and his wife Amber had decided, was just as good a name for a daughter as for a son. "And is Nanny okay?" Chrys asked.

"Yeah, about the same. She tries to wait to take her medicine at night so she's not so dopey during the day, but you can tell she's hurting. She's got a new girl staying with her now, though, so that helps a lot."

Chrys's grandmother was in remarkably good shape for her eighty-nine years, but a damaged hip and chronic arthritis kept her in a state of bearable but constant pain. Pain medication helped but made her spacey and forgetful, likely to leave the stove or an iron on. As a result of her mobility problems, it was a good idea for someone to stay with her, though Chrys knew Nanny found this loss of independence frustrating.

As was always the case, Chrys's mom summed up how everybody was without once saying how she herself was. It was like she was a cog in the machine of the family, and if the rest of the machine was all right, then she was, too. But a little worry crept into her voice at the end of the conversation. "You call me if you need anything at all, even if it's just to talk," she said.

"I will, Mom. I love you."

"Love you, too."

Chrys set the phone down. She had people who loved her. Her mom. Nanny. Aaron. But the absence of Meredith's love made her feel hollowed out, like a fish that's been gutted so it looks normal from the outside, but upon closer inspection, is an empty shell.

* * *

Waking up on a Monday morning to teach an eight o'clock English composition class was always a certain level of misery. But doing it in her current emotional state plumbed new depths. She shut off the alarm and lay there, barely awake, her mouth cottony, her hair unwashed all weekend, wondering how in the hell she could channel the teacher persona that answered to Ms. Pickett. She dragged herself out of bed, grabbed some clean clothes, and headed to the bathroom just as Aaron was heading out of it. He was wearing two towels, one around his waist and one around his head, turban-style. "No talky before coffee," he said, and Chrys nodded mutely.

She brushed her teeth, showered, brushed out her hair, and put on her old reliable light blue floral print dress. Applying her usual holy trinity of makeup—powder base, mascara and lipstick—helped her puffy eyes and pale complexion a little but not enough. She couldn't figure out why she felt like something was missing until she remembered the diamond earrings she had left on the dresser at the house. She was going to have to dig out the silver hoops that had been her go-to earrings before Meredith.

Aaron was sitting at the kitchen table with a cup of coffee and a bagel. "I left the bagels out if you want one."

"No, thank you," Chrys said, and to her embarrassment, she felt tears spring to her eyes, threatening her freshly applied mascara. "To be honest, I don't know if I can do this."

"Eat breakfast? Well, it is optional, though rumor has it it's the most important meal of the day."

"No, I don't think I can do any of this." She gestured vaguely. "Go to work. Function. Talk to people."

"I'm people, and you're talking to me." Aaron slathered the other half of his bagel with cream cheese.

"Yeah, but you're my sister. How do I talk to co-workers and students?"

"It's called acting, honeybun. Pretend you're in the thea-TAH. You're playing the role of an English professor who doesn't feel like she just had her heart stomped on by Godzilla."

Chrys filled a mug with coffee and wasn't reassured to see how much her hands were shaking. "You're the one who's good at pretending."

"Oh, you know better than that. How long did you manage to convince yourself you were straight despite ample evidence to the contrary?"

Aaron never forgot anything Chrys had told him, no matter how much wine they'd both had at the time of the telling. "Until I was twenty-two."

He smiled. "And how many more years after that did you let your parents think you were straight?"

"Eight." She had come out to her mom, and shortly thereafter, her dad, right before her thirtieth birthday, having decided that she didn't want to enter the third decade of her life as a de facto liar.

"Exactly! You're plenty good at pretending. And you won't even have to try that hard. Most people who look at you will see what they want to see anyway. And your students are probably too busy texting and updating their Facebook status to notice anything. Unless you collapse weeping on the podium when you're supposed to be giving a lecture on commas."

Chrys didn't tell Aaron that collapsing weeping on the podium seemed like a distinct possibility.

* * *

She pulled into the faculty parking lot, took a deep breath and said, "I can do this." Then she took another deep breath and said it again. When after the third time of saying it she still didn't believe it, she said "Fuck it" and opened the car door anyway.

She muttered good morning to a couple of colleagues she knew only in passing, a guy from the business department and a woman from nursing. Easy enough, but she knew once she entered the shared General Studies office, conversation would be unavoidable.

The only other instructor in her department with an eight o'clock class was Susan, who had the thankless job of teaching Introduction to College, which covered useful but hardly riveting topics such as study skills and time management. Susan was in her fifties, kept her hair cut short, and had the slightly butch quality of a high school gym teacher. In Chrys's opinion, Susan would have made an excellent lesbian, but appearances to the contrary, she had a husband at home.

Susan looked away from her computer screen, which was currently splashed with celebrity photos and lurid headlines. "How was your weekend?" she asked.

Chrys struggled for an answer. The easy way out would be to say fine, how about yours? But Susan was her best work buddy, one of the few people at Hill College who had genuinely shown an interest in her life. "Do you want the polite answer or the real answer?"

"Since when have you known me to be interested in the polite anything?" One of the objects on Susan's desk was a needlepoint sampler of the Alice Longworth Roosevelt line, *If you can't find anything nice to say, come sit by me.*

Chrys twirled around in her desk chair to face Susan. "Okay, then. I'm waiting for the government to declare my weekend a national disaster. Meredith broke up with me."

Susan looked genuinely shocked. "She did what? After you moved down here for her? What is she thinking?"

"She's thinking she found someone younger and prettier." Chrys felt a knot form in her throat. "But I can't talk about it much right now because I'll cry. And I can't cry because I have to teach."

"The students will just think you're crying because their papers are so bad. Seriously, though, I really am sorry. If there's anything I can do, let me know."

"Thanks, but I can't think of anything."

"Me neither." Susan turned back to her computer.

* * *

When Chrys walked into the classroom, she was privy to the usual pre-class student chatter, some of it about sports, some of it about family stuff, some—as was the case with the two girls in the front row—seemingly devoid of any content at all.

Girl 1: He did not!

Girl 2: He did!

Girl 1: Shut *up*!

Girl 2: I know, right?

The first time she said "Good morning," Chrys's voice came out weak and quavery. She took a deep breath and tried again. This time she was loud enough that the chatter started to die down. She felt the students' eyes on her. *Don't cry, don't run*, she told herself. "I want to go ahead and collect your descriptive essays," she said, trying to sound as calm and businesslike as possible. "Pass them down to the end of each row, please."

"Miss Pickett?" A furtive-acting student was standing beside her. Her green-shadowed eyes were shifty, and she was chipping at the hot pink polish on her fingernails. "Um… Miss?" She trailed off. "I did my paper, and I got it on my flash drive, but I can't open it on the computers here?" This student was clearly enrolled in the Rising Inflection School of Excuses.

Chrys knew at this point she was supposed to make some sound of agreement, but she chose not to.

"So I was wondering if I could turn it in tomorrow?"

"You may, but I'll have to deduct five points for lateness."

The girl put a pink-nailed hand to her chest as if the shock of this injustice was causing heart palpitations. "But I did it! It's on my flash drive!"

"And if you can get it off your flash drive and to me by five o'clock today, I won't take off any points." Sometimes she thought back fondly to her early days of teaching when students couldn't use technology as an excuse for not having their papers ready on time. Back then they had to think up real excuses—sick grandmothers, paper-munching dogs. At least they had to be creative.

Today her task was to introduce *The Great Gatsby*, of which her students had allegedly read the first thirty pages. She turned to the dry-erase board, mouthing "I can do this" once her back was turned, and wrote *The American Dream* in big letters. She turned around. "So, what are some of the things you think of when you hear the phrase 'the American Dream?'"

Silence except for the sound of the girl popping her gum in the front row.

Chrys wasn't in the mood to work this hard. "Okay," she said. "You're all here in a college classroom this morning instead of being cozy in bed, so you must be here because you're working toward some kind of goal. What are some of the goals you're working toward? Might any of those fall under the heading of the American Dream?"

Finally, after an uncomfortable silence, a girl in the back named Chelsea said, "A nice house."

"Yes," Chrys said, writing the answer on the board. "A nice house is always part of the American dream, right? Preferably with a white picket fence."

Haltingly, a few more students pitched in with "nice things," "plenty of money," and—from a gentleman in the back row—"a hot wife," which Chrys wrote on the board as "a desirable partner." Finally, some of the quietest students in the class pitched in with some more abstract ideas: happiness, security, love.

Chrys took a step back from the board and looked at the words that filled it: nice house, desirable partner, happiness, security, and love. Just like a character F. Scott Fitzgerald would have written about, she'd had it all and lost it all so fast she didn't know what had hit her. She swallowed back the ball of sadness in her throat and asked the students to turn to page one.

CHAPTER FOUR

It had been three weeks and one day since D-Day, as Chrys had come to call it. D-Day was short for Dump Day, a phrase with a scatological ring that Chrys found appropriately distasteful.

Her life at Aaron's had taken on a routine that she was able to drag herself through every day: wake up, shower, don teacher clothes, groom, caffeinate and ingest toast, and proceed to work where she did a robotlike but apparently credible impersonation of an English professor for the required number of hours. Then it was back to the apartment, to the couch, where she flopped, sometimes slept, sometimes stared at the TV, sometimes just stared. Nights when Aaron came home and they cooked dinner together things livened up a bit, especially if they opened a bottle of wine. But on nights when Aaron taught his improv class or went out with his tribe of guy friends, it seemed like she was counting the grains of sand sifting through a slow-motion hourglass. Those were the nights when she hit the red wine and chocolate ice cream pretty hard. She wasn't guzzling either substance enough to be a significant problem, unless the problem of zipping her jeans was significant.

The weekends were the hardest because they robbed her of a routine she could force herself to stick to. She knew she should create her own routine, but she lacked the energy. As a result, it was now two in the afternoon and she was lying on the couch, unshowered and in her rattiest sweatpants, watching a Food Network show that was making her hungry though she lacked the energy to get up and make a sandwich. Aaron had been out of the house for hours, no doubt doing all sorts of fun but meaningful activities. She thought, not for the first time, what a drag it must be to have her crashing here like this.

But there were only two more weeks until the spring semester was over, and then she was going to Do Something to Change Her Life. She thought about this change in capital letters to make it seem more decisive, but the truth was she had no idea what to do. Before Meredith (B.M., as she had come to call it, which also generated some scatological humor) she had envisioned two possible paths for her life. The first was that she would stay at Western Carolina and work her way up the professorial ranks. She would act as mentor to more than one generation of English majors, and she would publish work in journals and maybe even produce another book. Since the place wasn't exactly teeming with lesbians, her personal life would have suffered on this path, but a long-distance relationship would've been a possibility. The second path— the ideal one—was that a few years at Western Carolina would serve as a springboard to get her a job at a larger university in a more cosmopolitan area where she could have a stimulating academic career, meet someone, fall in love, and proceed to happily ever after.

But her relationship with Meredith had gotten her so far off course from her original plans that she felt like she was in the middle of a stormy ocean with no navigational tools to guide her.

The door swung open, startling Chrys from her brooding. "Hey," she said to Aaron.

"Fresh strawberries from the farmers market," he said, setting down a brown paper bag. "And look at you. You're right where I left you."

"Just like a houseplant." Suddenly Chrys felt hyper-aware of her unwashed hair and tragic sweatpants. "God, it must be a drag to come home and always find this dejected dyke on your couch."

Aaron sat down next to her. "You should say 'dejected dyke on your davenport.' That's what my grandma called couches, and it makes for better alliteration."

"Dejected dyke on your davenport, then."

"But don't be silly. I know you'd do the same for me if our roles were reversed. And if I ever managed to sustain enough of a long-term relationship for a breakup to really hurt." He patted her knee. "Hey, the callbacks for the Shakespeare on the Square production of *Midsummer Night's Dream* were today."

"And the part you got was…" She knew he wouldn't be in such a good mood if he hadn't been cast.

"I'm Bottom."

"Well, that borders on too much information. But then, I never took you for a top."

"You vicious bitch." Aaron laughed. "You have a PhD in English. You know damn well what I mean."

"Yes, I do. It's a great comic role."

"Yeah, but I've done Shakespeare on the Square before, and it's crazy. You're out there in the middle of the square surrounded by bars and restaurants. There are drunks and hecklers and children—"

"Just like the actors in Shakespeare's day had to put up with," Chrys said. "You can just pretend Elizabeth the First is in the audience."

"Well, if my friends come, there will definitely be some queens." Aaron reached into the paper bag. "Have you eaten? I bought a hunk of Havarti at the farmers market. It'll go great with the strawberries."

"No, I haven't eaten. Eating would require moving from this couch, which I've been too shiftless to do. But I solemnly swear that by the time *Midsummer Night's Dream* opens, I'll be off your couch for good. I don't know where I'll be, but it won't be here." As if to illustrate, she rose from the couch and followed Aaron into the little galley kitchen.

He got out a colander and started rinsing the strawberries. "It would be cool if you could find an apartment around here. We could go from roommates to neighbors."

Chrys set the wedge of Havarti on a plate with a knife and some of those table water crackers she liked even though they were largely tasteless. "That would be cool. I don't know, though. I feel like suddenly at the age of forty I've decided I don't know what I want to be when I grow up. I don't totally hate my job, but without Meredith, the job's just not enough, you know?"

They settled at the kitchen table—maybe because Aaron was trying to steer her away from the couch. "It would be nice if you could get a job at the university," Aaron said, then popped a strawberry into his mouth. "That way you could teach English majors—maybe even graduate students."

"Yeah, but hiring over there doesn't work like that." Chrys cut a sliver of Havarti and placed it on a cracker. "Even if the English department did have an opening, they'd do a national search, and I'd be way out of my league with that competition."

"Being a grownup sucks, huh?" Aaron gave a rueful smile and poured them some ginger ale since it was too early for wine. "So many compromised dreams. You know, when I was six years old, nobody could tell me that I wouldn't be the world's first black male Radio City Music Hall Rockette."

Chrys smiled. "Well, you do pretty well for yourself anyway."

"It could be worse. Massage therapy is a pleasant enough way to pay the bills, and I feel like I'm actually helping people. And I get to be in two or three local productions a year. But still, it's not exactly living the dream, is it?"

"Because you're not a Rockette?"

"No, because I'm not a professional actor," Aaron said, popping another strawberry. "You know, right after I graduated from UT, I moved to New York. I told myself I'd try it for a year to see if I could make it happen. I worked for a temp agency, shared a one-room apartment with two other people, and went to every audition I could. The only part I got was a non-paying role in this crazy performance piece that ran for four performances at a public school in Brooklyn. After a year of barely making my part of the rent and surviving on a bowl of oatmeal and a bowl of ramen a day, I came back to Knoxville on the Greyhound of Shame."

"You had no reason to be ashamed. You gave it your best shot."

He shrugged. "Yeah, but then I had to start compromising. I learned that a big part of being a grownup is deciding what you can live with."

"God, that's depressing," Chrys said, reaching for a strawberry. It burst in a sweet, juicy explosion in her mouth. "But one thing that makes me feel a little better is that these strawberries are really, really good."

* * *

Chrys was waiting in her car in the parking lot of the Country Cookin' Buffet. The CCB, as Chrys called it, was not her usual dining choice, but a couple of days earlier her mom had called saying it was time for Nanny's annual visit with her rheumatologist at UT Hospital. It was a two-and-a-half-hour drive from Piney Creek to Knoxville, which made it not only the longest trip Nanny made all year, but with the exception of one bus visit to Detroit in the 1960s, the longest trip Nanny had made in her life.

The yearly trip to Knoxville was a big deal for Nanny, and her post-appointment treat was always lunch at the Country Cookin' Buffet on Clinton Highway. The sign outside the restaurant said *All You Care to Eat*, which Chrys always found rather damning, as though the restaurant's proprietor was implying that given the quality of the food, you wouldn't care to eat much.

Mom pulled into the parking lot in Nanny's lane-hogging Oldsmobile, which dated from the eighties when Papaw was still alive. When Chrys and her brother Dustin were teenagers, they used to think it was hilarious that their then-ancient-seeming grandparents tootled around in an Oldsmobile. If Batman drives a Batmobile, they'd say, then what do old people drive?

The Oldsmobile squeezed into the parking space next to Chrys's, and her mom waved cheerfully. When Mom got out of the car, Chrys saw that the current do-it-yourself hair color was a not-found-in-nature burgundy, and her nails were painted to match. Mom would never pay for expensive highlights and a manicure at a salon, but she was a frequent visitor to the hair dye and nail polish aisles. Meredith (Chrys winced) always called Chrys's mom's look "drugstore femme." Chrys got out of the car and met her mom for a hug.

"Lord, I hate driving that old thing," Mom said. "Might as well bring your nanny in a tank. Her walker's in the back if you want to help with it."

"Sure," Chrys said, used to her mother's scattershot speech pattern.

Mom opened the front passenger door and Chrys steadied the walker. "Hi, Nanny," she said.

Nanny's silver hair was arranged in a cap of rigid curls—she always went to the beauty shop the day before her annual road trip. Giant hoot-owl glasses which would've been in style around the time the Oldsmobile was purchased framed her eyes, and she was wearing one of her three good dresses (this one peach) that signified a special occasion. "You come here and give me some sugar, child," she said, holding out her arms. "You look good. You've plumped up a right smart since I seen you last."

Chrys kissed Nanny's cheek. She knew Nanny had meant the acknowledgment of weight gain as a compliment; she always said thin women looked "poorly."

At the CCB, patrons had to pay upon entering to prevent them from pulling a dine and dash after having all they cared to eat. As always, Chrys offered to pay for Mom and Nanny's lunch and they held up the line by arguing with her for a couple of minutes but then relented.

Once the cashier unceremoniously handed them a pile of plates, Chrys helped Nanny through the buffet line, dipping whatever foods she indicated: fried chicken (which Chrys knew from experience was greasy on the outside and dry on the inside), instant mashed potatoes, canned green beans and corn. When they were seated and eating (the chicken pot pie wasn't bad, though Chrys suspected it was recycled from past-its-prime fried chicken), Chrys said, "Nanny, I never can figure out why you like this place so much. Not a single thing they have here is half as good as what you make." Nanny's cooking wasn't for the faint of heart—the amount of bacon grease she used would put anyone in danger of a bypass—but everything she cooked was delicious, and her chicken and dumplings were the stuff of legends.

"Well, I believe you just answered your own question," Nanny said, spooning up some corn. "None of this stuff is as good as what I cook, but I like it 'cause I didn't have to cook it. Plus, there's plenty of it, and when you came up like I did, sometimes it feels good to know you can eat till you're about to bust if you take a notion to."

Chrys smiled. "I can see that." Nanny was born at the height of the Depression. It was no wonder she liked a plentiful spread.

"Of course it ain't like I can cook the way I used to," Nanny said.

"I don't know," Mom said. "Them chicken and dumplings you made at Easter was the best I ever tasted. It was too bad you couldn't come, Chrystal."

Only Chrys's family called her by her given name. She had switched over to "Chrys" in college, finding her real name declasse, and was always quick to tell professors to call her Chrys before they called roll on the first day of class. "I wish I could've been there, too," she said. She and Meredith had spent the long Easter weekend in Key West, where Chrys had basked on the beach, innocent of the knowledge of Meredith's new girl.

"Well, maybe you can make it for Thanksgiving," Mom said. "That's the next time we'll put on a big feed."

"I should be able to," Chrys said. "It's not like my social calendar is exactly full these days."

"You know, that always used to puzzle me," Nanny said, gesturing with a chicken leg, "how a pretty girl like you could still have no husband and no young 'uns. But now I think I've got it figured out."

"Really?" Chrys exchanged glances with her mom. When Chrys had finally come out to her parents, her mom had been fine after a ten-minute crying jag, and her dad had been okay after a weekend-long fishing trip. But both Mom and Daddy had insisted that Chrys shouldn't tell Nanny about her sexuality. Nanny was of a different generation, and she was a Free Will Baptist. She wouldn't understand, they said, and it would just upset her. As a result, while Chrys had never told Nanny she was straight, she'd never told her she was gay either.

"You know what it is?" Nanny said, still using the chicken leg as a talking stick. "Men's scared of smart women. Unless you're dumb or act dumb, they run like scalded dogs. And I'm proud to have a granddaughter who ain't willing to play dumb just so she can get a man."

"Thank you, Nanny. So how did the doctor's appointment go?" Chrys was eager to shift the topic away from herself.

"It was all right, I reckon," Nanny said. "He wants me to do—what's it called, Joyce?"

"Physical therapy," Mom said. "He wrote a prescription for it and for more pain pills since we needed more after what happened."

"What do you mean?" Chrys pushed away her plate, having had all she cared to eat the first time around.

"We had to fire the last girl we had staying with your Nanny," Mom whispered as though the girl herself might be nearby. "She was stealing pills."

Chrys's jaw dropped. "She was stealing Nanny's pain medicine?" Nanny's rheumatoid arthritis kept her in constant pain. She stayed off the medication during most days, but she needed it at night so she could sleep.

"She was," Nanny said. "She was right sneaky about it at first, so I didn't catch on. She'd just sneak two or three pills out the bottle—enough that when I'd come up short I'd just think I'd counted them wrong. But then she got careless, and she'd take out a bunch of pills and replace them with mints thinking I'd not notice." She shook her head. "Now who with at least half their wits about them wouldn't know the difference between a pain pill and a mint? I'm old, but I ain't stupid."

"I don't know if she was taking the pills or selling them," Mom said. "But your brother told me druggies'll pay fifty bucks for one Oxycontin. I reckon she could make more money that way than what we could pay her to look after Nanny."

Chrys couldn't wrap her mind around the callousness of someone who would steal medication from an old person in pain in order to support a habit or turn a profit. "Did you have the girl arrested?"

"No, we just fired her and told her to be glad we didn't call the law," Mom said. A rueful smile crossed her lips. "And your brother told her she oughta be glad she's a woman because if any man was to do his nanny that way, he'd beat the hell out of him."

"I don't blame him," Chrys said. "I've got half a mind to beat up this girl myself."

"No, she already got what was coming to her," Nanny said. "Losing that job really tore her up. You know, she wasn't but twenty years old, and when Joyce fired her, she cried like a little girl. I told I'd pray for her, and I did."

"So now we're looking for somebody else to stay with Nanny," Mom said. "But it's hard to find somebody you can trust. If we could afford to hire a real nurse, it'd be different. But a lot of the people who'll work for what we can pay is the type who'd just take the job so they could get at the pain pills or whatever else there was to steal."

"That's rough," Chrys said. If she were still with Meredith, Meredith's deep pockets might be able to help with the problem. But on her own, Chrys's pockets were as shallow as an heiress with a purse dog.

"You know what?" Nanny said, reaching out for both her daughter's and granddaughter's hands. "I don't want us to spend our special time together talking about our worries. I think we ought to have something sweet. I've been dying to try that dessert bar ever since I heard they added a chocolate fountain."

Chrys didn't want to think about the germs that were surely lurking in the Country Cookin' Buffet's much dipped-in chocolate fountain. But she had always found Nanny's sweet tooth endearing. "Well, a chocolate fountain does seem like a pretty good place to drown your sorrows," she said.

CHAPTER FIVE

"Isn't the crown molding nice?" the perky young woman asked.

"Yes," Chrys said, though she wasn't the kind of person who noticed things like crown molding. On a whim, she had dropped by an apartment complex near work which displayed a balloon-bedecked sign advertising an open house. As soon as she entered the main office, she had been set upon by the perky blonde who introduced herself as Katie and was young enough to be one of Chrys's students. When Chrys had muttered that she might like to look at an apartment, Katie had smiled like she'd just won the lottery.

The "apartment home," as Katie insisted upon calling it, was fine—clean with a fresh coat of off-white paint and new tan carpet. There was a small living room with a sliding glass door leading to a balcony, a galley kitchen with a dining nook, and a bedroom and bathroom down the hall.

"Now if you'd like to see something a little less cozy, I can show you one of our two- or three-bedroom models," Katie said.

"No, thanks. I'll be living alone, though I might get a cat."
Chrys cringed, realizing that for Katie, she had just put herself
in the Lonely Middle-Aged Lady With Cat demographic.

"Pets are welcome," Katie said, "though there is a two
hundred dollar pet deposit. We also have some really neat
activities here. Every Tuesday is pizza night at the clubhouse,
and there's a racquet club and the pool."

Chrys hadn't heard the word "clubhouse" since
childhood—she was having a hard time not imagining it as a
rickety platform in a tree. "That's nice. Thanks for the tour.
I'll think about it and get back to you."

Katie pasted on an even wider smile. "Well, shouldn't we
just go ahead and fill out the application? The first month's
rent free deal expires after Friday."

"Then I'll get back to you on Friday if I'm interested."

On the way back to her car, a voice called, "Hey! Ms.
Pickett!"

Chrys turned around to see a buff, heavily tattooed student
who had barely managed to scrape out a C in her English
composition course last semester. "Hi, Brandon."

"So what are you doing here?" Brandon asked. He was
dressed in a wifebeater and shorts, perhaps on his way to the
"workout room" Katie had been so excited to tell her about.

"Oh, just looking at an apartment," Chrys said.

"Hey, that would be awesome!" Brandon said, with a smile
that reminded Chrys of a happily idiotic golden retriever.
"We'd be neighbors! We could hang out, slam a few beers."

Back at Aaron's, she poured herself a glass of red wine
and settled in her customary spot on the couch. What would
her life be like if she moved to Westview Manor Apartment
Homes? She'd buy a couch and a bed, maybe adopt a cat from
the Humane Society. But then what? She wasn't teaching this
summer, so the season yawned before her. She pictured long,
empty days in the plain little box of an apartment, lying on the
new couch or bed, aching with the loneliness of the rejected—a
loneliness that might drive her to go to the clubhouse for Pizza
Night or drink beer and play video games with her C student.

The only possible advantage to the situation was that she'd be on her own couch in her own apartment instead of Aaron's.

She carried her wineglass into the bedroom so she could change out of her teacher drag. As she reached into the drawer for a T-shirt, she remembered the box. Her mom had given it to her when they met for lunch the other day, and Chrys had set it down in her room where it disappeared among the other dozen cardboard boxes holding books and belongings. The contents of the box were covered with a towel, and she hadn't even bothered to look at them. Her mom usually gave her a boxload of stuff when she came to town, and it was never anything to get too excited about—clothes from yard sales, maybe a scented candle or a knickknack. Idly curious, she pulled back the box's covering and found a note in her mom's loopy handwriting:

We was cleaning out some stuff at Nanny's and found this box. Nanny thought you might like to have these things since you made them or made them with her help anyway. I know your going through a hard time right now and I'm sorry we couldn't talk about it in front of Nanny. Call me if you need to talk. Love, Mom

The first item in the box was a doll made out of a sweat sock. It was spectacularly ugly, with rainbow yarn hair, uneven button eyes, and a gash of red yarn for a mouth. If you hung it on somebody's door without an explanation, it would scare the shit out of them. Then there was a pillow made of sloppily stitched fabric with—it took Chrys a minute to remember the name of the character—Holly Hobby on it, and there were Christmas tree ornaments made out of a variety of children's arts and crafts media, dough and yarn and Popsicle sticks.

At first Chrys didn't realize she was sitting on the floor in tears, clutching a sock doll and a Holly Hobby pillow to her chest. If Aaron came home and found her like this, he'd have her committed. But crazy as she might look tearfully clutching items from her childhood, at least for the first time since D-Day she was crying about something other than Meredith.

Chrys's mom always had to work full-time. And so until she was school-age, she'd spent her days being looked after by

Nanny. Even after she was in school, the yellow bus dropped her at Nanny's, where she stayed until her mom picked her up at five thirty. In summer, she spent all day every day with Nanny, and Nanny always seemed happy to have her there.

Summers with Nanny were always full of projects: planting and tending the garden, picking blackberries and making jam, doing various craft projects that Chrys dreamed up. When they weren't working on something, they'd take turns reading to each other: Nanny would read from the newspaper, and Chrys would read from one of the library books she devoured. When the weather was so hot they felt extra lazy, they'd watch daytime TV, game shows or the soap operas that Nanny called "my stories."

Chrys cried not just because of the good care Nanny had given her, but because Nanny had no one to take care of her now that she needed it. How unfair that a woman who had spent the majority of her life caring for the people around her now had to depend on the likes of a girl who had no qualms about stealing an old lady's pills and replacing them with Tic Tacs.

Chrys set down the sweat sock and the Holly Hobby pillow that was now damp with her tears. She picked up the phone. For the first time since D-Day, she knew what she needed to do.

CHAPTER SIX

"Are you sure you want to do this?" Aaron was sitting cross-legged on the bed while Chrys packed her suitcase.

"I told myself I'd keep track of how many times you asked me that question," Chrys said, grabbing a handful of panties and stuffing them in the overpacked case. "But I've officially lost count. Let's just call the number infinity."

"I know I keep asking." Aaron was petting Miss Celie as he talked. "It's just that you don't see me running back to Niota, Tennessee, do you?"

"I'm only running back for the summer to take care of Nanny until we can find somebody responsible to take over. And I don't know—I think it'll be good for me to unplug for a while. I feel like I need to cut some ties here to get my life back together. I got rid of the expensive phone Meredith gave me and bought a little throwaway so just you and my folks will have the number. There's no Internet connection at Nanny's, so I'll be free of email. Maybe out in the country I'll be able to hear myself think, and make some sense of my life. I mean, what would I do if I stayed here all summer with no classes to teach? I'd just wallow in self-pity."

"That's not true," Aaron said. "You'd wallow in self-pity *and* come see me in *A Midsummer Night's Dream.*"

"I'll still come see you in *A Midsummer Night's Dream.* It's just two and a half hours from Piney Creek to Knoxville. And that road goes both ways, mister." She tossed a purple lacy bra from her underwear drawer at Aaron. "You can always come visit me if you want a bucolic weekend."

"Funny, as somebody who grew up as the gay kid in the only black family in a wide-place-in-the-road small town, I don't seem to crave bucolic weekends much." He tossed the bra back at her.

"I know this is hard for you to understand, but I just feel like it's the right thing for me to do. You should've heard Mom when I told her my idea. She was surprised and…touched, you know? She couldn't stop crying."

"I'm absolutely convinced that what you're doing is a nice person thing to do," Aaron said. "However, I'm not absolutely convinced that it's a sane person thing to do."

She had to admit he had her there. "I'm not either."

* * *

It didn't take long to get away from the city. Chrys was just a few minutes from Knoxville, and already the urban and suburban sprawl had been replaced by long stretches of nothing but trees and mountains. Parts of the road were framed by rock faces from back when the hills had been blasted apart to build the highway. The interstate exits were few and far between, but each one seemed to have a garishly advertised fireworks store.

As she drew nearer to the Kentucky state line, she passed a huge corrugated aluminum building labeled *Adult World* and decorated with poorly rendered silhouettes of buxom women. On the lot adjacent to the store was a huge white cross, also made of aluminum, which had been erected by an evangelical church to protest the porn store's presence. This pairing always struck Chrys as particularly Southern, the way sin and salvation sat right next door to each other with no middle ground in between. They seemed to offer passersby a choice: the Sign of the Cross or the Sign of the Crotch, take your pick.

Given the number of 18-wheelers in the Adult World parking lot, today the crotch was winning.

A sign marking the last exit before the Kentucky state line read *Last Chance Cold Beer*. But the sign seemed like another kind of warning: last chance to decide if her summer plan was a terrible idea and to turn the car around. She kept moving forward.

To get to Piney Creek, you had to exit the interstate and get on a state highway for twenty minutes and then turn left onto a winding but paved country road. Around the first curve of this country road was the Piney Creek Church of God, where you turned so abruptly as to feel like you were dropping off the face of the earth, ending up on a gravel road which turned into a dirt road. The first time Chrys gave Meredith directions to her family's home, she said, "You basically drive to nowhere and then keep turning left."

Chrys's family's house was nearly at the end of the holler. While small, the house had quite a bit of acreage with it, some of which was a nearby mountain. Chrys pulled into the long, curving, gravel driveway and heard the sound she most associated with visits home: the chorus of barks, from the soprano yipping of the Chihuahuas to the baritone baying of the hounds. Her parents never had fewer than six dogs, and right now it was looking more like eight as the Chihuahuas and hounds and a couple of unfortunate-looking Chihuahua-hound mixes ran alongside the wheels of the car, barking for all they were worth.

The Chihuahua-hound mixes had resulted a couple of years earlier when Chrys's mom had gotten a new Chihuahua around the same time Chrys's dad got a new hunting dog. The Chihuahua was apparently quite the Latin lover, and he had gotten to the hound before Chrys's parents had managed to have either dog fixed. The resulting litter had been an unappealing mash-up of Chihuahua and hound genetic traits, and as adults they were downright hideous. One resembled a flop-eared Chihuahua on stilts, while the other had the body of a hound but the pop eyes and bat ears of a Chihuahua. They looked like they'd been spliced together on the island of Dr. Moreau, and Chrys always called them the Chihoundhounds.

The house looked the same degree of run-down as it had since she was a teenager, the white aluminum siding dirtied to a dingy gray, concrete blocks standing in for the porch steps that Daddy had torn out with the intention of replacing before he lost his arm. In the backyard sat the ugly cream and olive green trailer that housed Dustin and his family. Such backyard trailers were a common sight in the area. Some homes in the country were surrounded by three or four trailers, like sharecroppers' shacks spread around the plantation house. But in this case the "sharecroppers" were the adult children of the homeowners.

As soon as Chrys parked the car, the door of the house swung open. There wasn't much chance of sneaking up unheard here. Mom ran out on the porch in one of the flowered muu-muus she favored for at-home wear in the summer. Her smile was wide. "There you are!" she said, meeting Chrys in a hug. "I can't believe you're doing this. You didn't even come home for the summer when you was in college."

It was true. Once Chrys had tasted life outside the holler her freshman year of college, she couldn't imagine going back. She had worked a part-time job and taken a class every summer so she could stay in the dorm. "Well, it's good to be here," she said, even if she wasn't quite sure yet if this was true or not.

"We got the extra room at Nanny's all ready for you," Mom said, "and I fixed us some dinner to have over there."

Chrys could tell it had been a long time since she'd been home because it took her a second to recalibrate to a setting where *dinner* meant *lunch*.

"Sissy!" Dustin, dressed in a pair of faded Levi's and nothing else, had appeared beside them. He had the same brown-as-a-berry tan he'd had as a little boy, though he was well muscled now and slight crow's feet had appeared beside his blue eyes. His chestnut hair hung past his shoulders. He was, as he had been since high school, a hillbilly Adonis.

"Hey, bro," she said, leaning in for a hug. It was the first time in over twenty years she'd had her arms around a shirtless man. As soon as she pulled away, she was startled by a tug on her shirt, the source of which could've been a Chihoundhound. But when she looked down, it was her niece Peyton, wearing cutoffs, a pink bikini top and a rhinestone tiara that glistened atop her golden curls. "Wow, Peyton, look how big you've gotten!" She knew this statement was straight out of the book of aunt cliches, but she couldn't help herself. The last time she'd seen Peyton, she'd been a little fireplug of a toddler. Now she was a little girl.

"I'm four now," Peyton announced.

"Aunt Sissy knows you're four," Dustin said, as Peyton hugged his leg. "You remember that pretty book she sent you on your birthday?"

"I spilled Mountain Dew on it, and it got all sticky," Peyton said.

Dustin grinned. "You wasn't supposed to tell that part."

Chrys smiled at her niece. "That's okay. I spill stuff on my books all the time. Coffee, usually."

Looking at Peyton, Chrys felt a flood of fondness for her, but also a flood of regret that she hadn't spent more time with her. When Chrys and Meredith had traveled, Chrys had always made it a point to buy gifts for Peyton: a tiny "I love New York" T-shirt, a plush bear dressed as a Beefeater, a Mexican marionette. She had thought of these gifts as a way of opening up the world to a little girl living in an eastern Kentucky holler. But now as Chrys stood before Peyton, she just felt like the kind of aunt who sends things but never visits.

"Well, you want to head up to Nanny's?" Mom asked Chrys. "We can have a bite to eat and get you settled in."

"Sure," Chrys said, "I'll take my car so I can unload my luggage."

"I wanna ride in the car with Aunt Sissy!" Peyton pronounced *aunt* as *aint*. Before Chrys could say anything, Peyton had the car door open and was sitting in the front passenger seat.

"Uh...shouldn't she be in the back in a car seat or something?" Chrys said.

Dustin laughed. "Shoot, Nanny's is just one field over from here. How bad a wreck could you get in? You've always worried too much."

Chrys thought, *And you've never worried enough.*

Nanny's house was small and boxy, with concrete statues of a kissing Dutch boy and girl in the front yard. If Chrys had to swerve to avoid Chihoundhounds in her parents' driveway, she had to swerve to avoid chickens here. Chrys didn't know if Nanny was familiar with the term "free-range chicken," but even if she didn't know the meaning of the phrase, she was still putting it to use. The birds were all over the yard, pecking and clucking and walking with that strange head-bobbing motion that reminded her of Mick Jagger dancing.

"Nanny kilt her one of them chickens at Thanksgiving," Peyton said.

"I heard she made chicken and dumplings," Chrys said, managing to park the car without flattening any fowl.

"Yeah, she did," Peyton said, "but first she had to kill her a chicken. I watched when she done it."

"Really?" As a child it hadn't taken Chrys long to realize she was too soft-hearted and squeamish for farm life. "Did it make you sad?"

"No," Peyton said, like Chrys had said something ridiculous. "It was funny. She wrung his neck, like this." She brought her hands together and simulated the twisting motion that had been the downfall of many a chicken. It was a strange move to see performed by a little girl wearing a tiara.

As Chrys made her way up the little pebble path to the house, her dad burst out the front door and said, "There's my baby girl!"

Peyton ran up to him and threw her arms around him. "Hi, Papaw!"

He smiled at Chrys, letting her know that Peyton hadn't been the baby girl he was addressing. Dad was wearing his "uniform": a green John Deere cap, old jeans, and a plain white Hanes T-shirt with one sleeve empty thanks to a logging accident years ago.

Once Chrys made it onto the porch, he draped his one arm around her in a half-hug. "So you're thinking you'll stay the whole summer?" His words were a little slurred because however big an occasion Chrys's homecoming was, it didn't merit him putting in his dentures.

"If you'll have me," Chrys said.

"Hell, if it was up to me, I'd put a trailer in the back for you right next to Dustin's. But I know that wouldn't suit you. You always had more gumption than he did."

"Yeah, but he got all the charm." Chrys watched Peyton chase a chicken across the yard. She hoped the little girl wasn't planning on putting her neck-wringing skills to work.

"Listen," Daddy whispered, his arm draped over Chrys's shoulder, "I was real sorry to hear about your friend doing you thataway. If she'd been a feller, I'd be half a mind to drag her behind my truck."

"Thanks, Daddy." Chrys was genuinely touched to hear her father acknowledge her breakup with Meredith. Like lots of her daddy's pronouncements, this one had a kind of hillbilly gallantry. He would think nothing of dragging a cheating lover behind a truck, if only she weren't a woman.

Nanny was in the living room in her La-Z-Boy recliner, wearing one of the floral print shifts she favored at home. "There's my new roommate!" she called.

Chrys leaned over and kissed Nanny's cheek. "That's right. We're going to get into all kinds of trouble."

Nanny cackled. "You hear that, Joyce? Chrystal's gonna lead me down the road to perdition."

Dustin laughed. "You'uns'll be partying so hard we'll hear it all the way down the holler. There'll be beer cans all over the yard, music cranking."

Chrys wondered what kind of music Nanny would crank. Gospel, probably, or one of her old Conway Twitty LPs.

The kitchen table was spread with a jumbo bag of off-brand potato chips, a loaf of white bread, a jar of Miracle Whip, and a plate of the kind of "lunch meats" Chrys hadn't thought of, let alone eaten, in decades: bologna, pickle loaf, olive loaf—all of them strangely pink, smooth, and symmetrical. Thankfully, there was also a stack of individually wrapped American cheese slices, and Chrys elected to forgo her cheese snobbery and make herself a processed cheese-food sandwich. She wasn't a vegetarian, but she drew the line at eating meat she couldn't readily identify.

Once they were settled around the table or leaning against the counter with their paper plates and plastic cups of Pepsi or Mountain Dew (or tap water, in Chrys's case), Nanny said, "There was a time when I'd have been plumb ashamed to serve the likes of this."

"There ain't nothing wrong with cold sandwiches in the summertime," Chrys's mom said, "and you don't need to be up on your feet cooking all morning."

"Besides, it's too hot to eat much anyhow," Dustin said, though he was already plowing through his second sandwich. His teenage appetite had never disappeared, and to Chrys's envy, neither had his teenage metabolism.

"I just wish I had something better to offer Chrystal, is all," Nanny said, picking at her potato chips. "Seems like with her coming home after all this time we ought to have killed a fatted calf or something."

Chrys smiled. So that's what she was—the prodigal daughter. "I don't eat veal anyway." She pried the gooey white bread from the roof of her mouth with her tongue. "A cheese sandwich is fine."

"I like baloney better'n cheese," Peyton said. She had eaten one half of her sandwich down to the crusts, which she had abandoned. "It's pink, so it's princess food."

Everybody laughed at bologna being such a royal dish. When Chrys and her mom were clearing the table, Daddy said, "When you're done, punkin, why don't you come outside with me? Nanny can tell you what she needs help with around the house, but I need to show you a couple of things outside."

Chrys smiled at how easily her daddy slipped into calling her by her childhood pet name. "Okay."

"I wanna go outside, too!" Peyton said, jumping up and down.

"Well, come on then, Princess Bologna," Chrys said. She was gratified when the little girl giggled.

Once they were out on the porch, Daddy said, "Now Dustin'll come up and mow the grass once a week, so you ain't got to worry about that. But you'll need to gather the eggs and feed and water the chickens. You remember how to do that?"

"I just sprinkle the chickens with a watering can, right?"

Peyton giggled again. "Aunt Sissy's silly!"

Daddy grinned. "No, your Aunt Sissy's a smart aleck. Always was, even when she was littler than you."

Daddy took her to the coop and showed her where the chicken feed was kept and how to fill the water dispenser. A red hen roosting in the coop clucked ill-temperedly.

"Now you hush up, Tinkerbell," Daddy said. "Ain't nobody gonna bother your eggs right now."

"The chicken's named Tinkerbell?" Chrys said.

"Yeah, Peyton names 'em all." Daddy took out his pouch of Red Man chewing tobacco.

"Uh-huh," Peyton said, rocking on the balls of her feet. "That's Tinkerbell, and then there's Snow White and Sleeping Beauty and Cinderella and Belle. There was Ariel, too, but we ate her."

"The rooster's Prince Charming," Daddy said, stuffing a pinch of tobacco in his jaw.

It was hard to think of anything less Disney-princess-like than these dopey, dumpy chickens, but Chrys had no doubt that Peyton would outfit them all in tiny tiaras if she could.

"So that'll take care of the chickens," Daddy said as they walked the path past the coop. "And back here we've got Porkchop."

Lying on his side, snoring through his snout, was a big pink hog. It had long been an annual custom to Chrys's family to raise a hog which they would butcher in the winter. As a kid, Chrys had always tried to find someplace else to be on butchering day. "And what do I have to do for Porkchop?"

"Just throw him some slop of a morning. Your nanny keeps a bucket in the kitchen for potato peelings and scraps. Just mix that up with some water, and he'll be happy. Dustin'll feed him in the evening and clean out his pen, so you don't have to worry about that."

"His poop stinks," Peyton said.

"I'm sure it does," Chrys said.

"But you know what he likes?" Peyton picked up a long stick, poked it between the slats of the pen, and used it to scratch the hog's back. In his sleep, he grunted with pleasure.

Chrys knew she'd have a hard time feeding, let alone scratching, Porkchop, knowing his fate. It would be like befriending a prisoner on death row. At least she'd be long gone by the time his execution date rolled around.

Once they were back in the house, Chrys's mom oriented her as to what pills Nanny took when, what doctor's appointments she had, when the physical therapist was supposed to come. Soon everybody cleared out so Nanny could nap, and Chrys was left to get settled.

Her room was tiny, just big enough for the maple bed and chest of drawers that had been there since before Chrys was born. On the bed was a worn-thin chenille bedspread which Chrys could remember falling asleep on when she was little. She'd always wake up with the bedspread's designs embedded in her face. The room's only decoration was an old, sentimental picture of two children crossing a bridge while being watched over by a guardian angel. The room was as frozen in time as an insect preserved in amber. It was strange being here, even stranger because it was strange and familiar at the same time. She wasn't sure how she felt about being here yet, but she did know one thing: today had contained the longest period of time that she had gone without thinking of Meredith since D-Day. And that at least was something.

CHAPTER SEVEN

When Chrys got up at seven, Nanny was already awake and sitting in her recliner. "You beat me," Chrys said. "I was trying to be the early bird, but I guess you got the worm."

"I never can sleep later than six o'clock." Nanny fiddled with the TV remote. "When Chester was alive, I always had to get up at five thirty to fix his breakfast. Even though he's been gone more than thirty years, I still can't break the habit."

Chrys's papaw died when she was eight years old. Even though she'd heard her mom comment on his love of beer joints and his hot temper, he'd never been anything other than sweet to her. "And now you're going to have to get into the habit of me fixing breakfast for you. You'll have to be patient with me, though. I'm not the cook that you are."

"Well, I ain't the cook that I used to be," Nanny said, smiling at the compliment. "I ain't the eater I used to be either. Whatever you want to fix will be all right with me."

"Breakfast food's pretty hard to screw up. What do you usually have?"

"Oh, not much. Just coffee, a couple of pieces of bacon, a biscuit or two, and a fried egg flipped over. I never could stand sunny side up eggs…feels like they're kinda staring at you."

Since Chrys was usually a cup-of-yogurt-and-a-coffee kind of girl in the morning, Nanny's breakfast order was daunting. "I'm not sure I can handle the biscuits, Nanny."

Nanny grinned. "Oh, I don't mean scratch biscuits. I just make those when I'm feeding somebody besides me. They's some canned biscuits in the Frigidaire."

"Those I can handle."

The kitchen was still decked out in the shades of the seventies: avocado refrigerator and stove, aging earth-tone linoleum, wallpaper printed with burnt orange and harvest gold coffeepots. She rummaged around for a minute, looking for the pans, until the memory of where Nanny had always kept things returned. She put the coffee on, opened the can of biscuits with a satisfying pop, and got out the bacon and eggs. She couldn't remember the last time she'd fried bacon or an egg for that matter, but she slapped the pans on the stove and hoped for the best. The bacon lay in the pan, limp and pale and unappetizing, until it finally started to sizzle. She broke the yolk of the first egg as soon as she cracked the shell. The second egg's yolk didn't break until she tried to flip it in the pan. When the third one broke, she whispered "fuck it" and finished cooking it anyway. She wasn't going to waste a dozen eggs trying to fry one properly even if the yard was full of chickens.

It took the bacon longer than she'd anticipated to get crispy, and by the time she got the biscuits out of the oven, crispy had given way to burnt. And of course, the broken-yolked fried egg had been done for a while, giving it ample time to grow cold and congealed. She set up a TV tray for Nanny in front of her recliner. "Your breakfast is ready," she said, "but once you get a look at it, I wouldn't blame you if you sent me packing back to Knoxville."

Nanny said, "I'm sure it's fine, honey," but when Chrys actually set the plate in front of her, she laughed. "When your mommy and her sisters was little, they always liked to make me breakfast for Mother's Day. This kindly puts me in mind of what they used to fix."

"Sorry," Chrys said.

"Don't be sorry. You made me remember something nice. Besides, I've always been partial to burnt bacon. Why don't you get yourself something, too? You need to keep up your strength to look after the likes of me."

"I already feel like I'm not doing a good enough job taking care of you." She didn't want to cry, but she felt a telltale tickle in the back of her throat.

"Pshaw!" Nanny said, reaching out to take Chrys's hand. "Do you know what a comfort it is to have you here with me instead of some stranger who steals my pills? I'd rather have burnt bacon cooked by you than perfect bacon cooked by a thief any day."

Chrys grabbed a cup of coffee and a biscuit (the one part of the meal she had managed not to screw up), sat in front of the TV, and watched a parade of inanities on the morning show: soft-pedal interviews, watered-down news, low-fat recipes, the weather. Much more entertaining was Nanny's running commentary. "I don't think that woman ever draws a sober breath," she said of one hostess. And then there was "You know, that colored man used to be as big as the side of a house."

When the show was over, Chrys said, "Now your physical therapist is coming at eleven. I thought I'd go wash the breakfast dishes. Is there anything else I can do to help out before your appointment?"

"Well, I kindly hate to ask you, but it's gotten hard for me to get in and out of the bathtub by myself. I've been making due with sponge baths mostly, but I'm starting to feel like I need a good soaking."

Lots of Chrys's students worked low-paying jobs in nursing homes, feeding and washing elderly patients, toileting or diapering them. Chrys was always thankful that there were people in the world who could perform such messy, intimate ministrations, but she had never thought of herself as one of them. If her students could bathe elderly strangers, surely she could manage with her own grandmother. "I'll go fill the tub."

"If you don't care, put some of them Calgon bath beads in it. They're under the sink."

As Chrys filled the tub, she tried to look at the bathroom from the point of view of someone with limited mobility. It was a nightmare. There was no shower, just a deep tub. The toilet was in the corner, its low height less than ideal for someone with trouble getting up and down. She adjusted the water temperature from hot to warm and watched as the bath salts turned the water an unnatural shade of blue.

In the living room, she said, "It's ready, Nanny. Want me to help you up?"

"Just hand me my walker, child."

"I think it's funny that you still call me 'child.'"

"If I can remember when you was a child and I wasn't a child myself at the time, then you're a child." She groaned as she pulled herself up on her walker.

"In that case, I'll be a child," Chrys said. "Being a grownup is no picnic."

"It ain't," Nanny said. "And being old's a downright pain in the hind end."

"You know what they say, though. It's better than the alternative."

Nanny laughed. "There's something to that, I reckon." In the bathroom, she seemed suddenly shy. "You think you could help me out of my things?" She lifted her arms like a little kid, and Chrys pulled up her nightgown. "I can take care of the step-ins myself," Nanny said. "I have a harder time getting them on than taking them off." She pushed her voluminous white panties down her hips and let gravity do the rest of the work. She cast her gaze down at the floor. "I don't reckon you've ever seen a nekkid eighty-nine-year-old woman before."

"No, I haven't." There was no point in pretending not to notice. She had to pay attention to Nanny's body to get her into the tub safely.

"Well, this is what you have to look forward to."

Actually, Chrys thought, Nanny's body did look like what Chrys's elderly body might. Nanny had always been on the curvy side like Chrys, but the parts that were still full and rounded on Chrys had flattened and sagged on Nanny. The effect was an overall softening, like an overripe piece of fruit. It lacked the suppleness of youth, but had its own beauty. How strange that the elderly human body was kept so hidden, so mysterious. Young bodies were on display all the time, reminding middle-aged women what they had once been, but there were no images to show them what they would become. "I hope I'm lucky enough to get to have an eighty-nine-year-old body."

"Well, it ain't the same as a twenty-nine-year-old body, but any age is a good age to be." She positioned herself beside the tub. "Usually what I do is set down on the edge of the tub and kindly turn myself around."

"Okay." Chrys took Nanny's arms and helped lower her to a sitting position. The process of getting her turned and lowered into the water was a slow, stop-and-go affair, with Nanny sometimes grimacing in discomfort, but once Nanny was settled, she sighed and said, "Now that feels good."

"Do you need it colder or hotter?"

"You could make it a little hotter, I reckon. Heat up these old bones." She looked down at herself. "The women in our family was always filled out. Not fat, just..."

"Voluptuous?"

"Well, I don't know about that," Nanny said, smiling. "That word sounds kindly dirty, don't it? Now when Chester and me first got married he always said I had an hourglass figure. But really, he just meant I had big titties and a big hind end. I never had the little waist for an hourglass. If my figure had been an hourglass, the sand would've run through a lot faster than an hour."

"Same here," Chrys said, laughing. When she was in college, she had gone through a phase of wanting a lithe, athletic figure like the tomboy dykes she was always attracted to. But then she discovered that the tomboys liked her curves, so she learned to like them, too.

"If you'll hand me a washrag, I can take care of things from here," Nanny said. "I'll just need help when it's time to get out."

"How about I check back on you in ten minutes or so? That'll give you some time to soak."

Chrys started the breakfast dishes. Seeing Nanny naked and helping her into the tub had been less awkward than she'd thought it would be. She wondered if it was healthier to live in a society where nudity wasn't so taboo, where seeing friends and family members' bodies was no big deal, where there was no embarrassment about breast-feeding or skinny-dipping or helping an old lady into a tub. She wasn't going to become a nudist any time soon—paying for all that sunscreen would get expenisve—but still, it was undeniable that turning the multi-purposed human body into a private, sexual thing came at a cost.

It had been a long time since Chrys had washed dishes, and the mindless, repetitive nature of it was strangely soothing. When she lived with Meredith, the dinner dishes would wait in the sink each morning until the maid arrived. It was amazing how quickly Chrys had fallen into the habit of letting someone else clean up after her. Amazing and a little scary.

When Chrys returned to the bathroom, Nanny's cheeks were flushed pink from the hot water. "Do you need me to help you wash your hair?" Chrys asked.

"No, honey, I get it warshed on Saturday at the beauty shop."

Chrys had forgotten the old-lady tradition of the Saturday morning shampoo-and-set, which got the coiffure in good order for church on Sunday. She had no problem taking Nanny to get her hair done, but she hoped she wouldn't have to take her to church. "Are you ready to get out?"

It took a good while to help Nanny out of the tub and into her bra and panties and the pink tracksuit Joyce had bought her to wear for physical therapy. It was the first time Chrys had ever seen Nanny wearing pants. "You never know," Nanny said, looking down at her athletic gear. "When that feller gets here, he might make me run all the way down the holler."

"Well, you'd better rest up then. Or have a second cup of coffee."

"I think I'll do both."

Once Nanny was settled back in her recliner, cup in hand, Chrys took a few minutes to make herself presentable. She changed into a fresh T-shirt and a pair of cargo shorts, washed her face, brushed her teeth, and pulled her hair back into a ponytail. She didn't bother with jewelry or makeup because it was just her and Nanny. Who was she trying to impress? The chickens? The chickens! She hadn't fed them or the pig yet. The demands of rural life were going to take some getting used to. "I've got to go take care of the critters," she told Nanny.

"They's some stale cornbread on the back of the stove. If you crumble it up with some buttermilk, Porkchop likes it real good."

Chrys had heard the expression "madder than a wet hen" before, but right now "madder than a hungry hen" was more fitting. The chickens were apparently unaccustomed to breakfasting at a late hour, and they squawked and flapped their wings irritably as Chrys opened their bag of feed. A little black banty rushed at her and pecked at her tennis shoes in an apparent attempt to get her to move faster. "Jesus, haven't you girls heard of brunch before?" Chrys scattered the cracked corn on the ground. The chickens jockeyed for position, nudging each other out of the way to peck at the kernels. She let them have at it, picked up her bucket of cornbread-buttermilk slurry, and proceeded to the pen of the porcine prisoner.

As soon as Porkchop spotted her—or, more likely, spotted the bucket—he started squealing and oinking up a storm. His curly little tail quivered in anticipation.

"Hungry, buddy?" Chrys said, then reminded herself not to fraternize with the doomed inmate. She poured the slop in his trough, and he fell to immediately, snorting, slurping and smacking. Chrys knew the little bit of farmwork she'd just done was a tiny fraction of what Nanny did growing up, tending a big garden, caring for pigs and chickens and cows—feeding things so they would feed you. She thought of her students, whose idea of food preparation was microwaving a Hot Pocket. It was good that everybody didn't have to work as hard as Nanny did growing up, but there was something to be said for knowing how to do things the hard way.

When Chrys came back in the house, Nanny was on the phone. "Here she comes," she said. "She can tell you." Nanny covered the mouthpiece with her hand. "It's the physical therapist. And she's a girl," she said, like she was announcing the birth of a baby. "She needs directions."

Chrys took the phone from Nanny.

"Hi, this is Dee, the girl physical therapist." It was a warm, good-humored voice. "I think I've gotten myself lost. I'm at the end of the holler outside a trailer that has a bunch of hound dogs in pens in the backyard." As if on cue, hounds bayed in the background.

"You've gone too far."

"That's not the first time somebody's said that to me."

Chrys laughed. "Well, in this case, it's an easy problem to fix. Just get yourself turned around, and then take the first driveway on the left."

Dee the Girl Physical Therapist was a few inches taller than Chrys. She had the natural tan of an outdoorsy type and wavy hair the color of toasted wheat which she wore in a braid down her back. Her green polo shirt bore a crest reading Mountainview Physical Therapy. "Thanks for the directions," she told Chrys. "I really should get a GPS, but I hate that little voice bossing me around."

"It's always such a smarmy little voice, too," Chrys said. The GPS in Meredith's Lexus always gave directions in clipped, BBC-perfect English. "I'm Chrys, by the way. Come on in and meet Nanny."

"That's not my name, you know," Nanny called from her chair.

"Dee, this is my grandmother, Mrs. Dottie Simcox. Nanny, is that an acceptable introduction?"

"That was much better. Just 'cause I'm your nanny don't make me Nanny to everybody." She looked in Dee's direction and smiled. "Nice to meet you, honey."

Dee moved closer to Nanny and shook her hand. "Nice to meet you, too. We're going to see if we can get you up and moving around some today."

Dee's use of the hospital "we" notwithstanding, Chrys was feeling like the third wheel in this equation, so she excused herself to her room. She stretched out on the chenille bedspread and opened the collection of short stories she was reading, her concentration broken occasionally by Dee's voice or Nanny's grunts or groans.

Dee didn't seem like someone who would spend her days winding through the hills and hollers. Her look and her grammar seemed like what Chrys's dad would half-jokingly call "citified." Chrys told herself to concentrate on her book. Since the breakup, her concentration had suffered terribly. She especially hated how this lack of focus affected her reading, which for as long as she could remember had been as important to her as eating and sleeping.

When Dee called that they were finished, Chrys found Nanny sitting in her recliner with a bottle of water.

"I believe I wore her out today," Dee said, smiling. "But remember what I said, Mrs. Simcox. The more you stretch, the easier it'll get."

"Don't let this girl's pretty face fool you," Nanny said, nodding in Dee's direction. "She's tough as a cob."

"Well, you're no marshmallow yourself, Mrs. Simcox." Dee turned to Chrys. "I told your nanny I might want to take a quick look around the house to see if I could make a few suggestions about things that might make her daily activities a little easier."

"That would be great," Chrys said. "The bathroom seems to be especially problematic."

"Well, let's have a look." Dee followed Chrys to the bathroom and surveyed it. "Well, right now I'd say the only thing you could do to make it worse would be to throw some banana peels on the floor."

"It is pretty bad, isn't it?" Chrys said, feeling strangely embarrassed. "I've just been staying here since yesterday, and helping her into the tub this morning was—"

"Terrible for both of you, I'm sure. She needs a shower stall with a seat and some railing other than that flimsy towel rack to help her get on and off the toilet. Medicare should pay for it if her doctor and I recommend it. And you don't need to be lifting a full-grown woman in and out of the tub, or pretty soon you'll need physical therapy yourself."

When they came out of the bathroom, Nanny said, "Now Chrystal, you walk her out when she's ready to go, all right?"

"Yes, ma'am."

When they were out on the porch Dee said, "Every single house I go to around here, the old people worry about not being able to walk me out. It's like they're afraid I won't be able to find my way back to my car."

"My parents always insisted on walking people out, too," Chrys said. "It's an Appalachian thing. Politeness is big here. Except when it's not."

Dee laughed. "I know what you mean."

Chrys's curiosity was getting the best of her. "I'm going to ask you a very Appalachian question if you don't mind."

"Shoot." Dee made full eye contact, and Chrys noticed that her eyes were very blue.

"You're not from around here, are you?"

Dee flashed a wide, easy grin. "Your nanny asked the same thing, except she said 'ain't.' The answer is I am but I'm not. I was born here, but my dad got a job in Cincinnati when I was three, and we moved there. My brother can remember living here, but I can't. But we always came here and stayed at my grandparents' for Christmas, and then we'd drive down for the Fourth of July and stay two weeks. My brother always hated it. He got bored and missed playing ball with his friends, but I always liked how much room there was to wander off by myself and imagine things."

Chrys nodded. "That was my favorite part about growing up in the country. There was a lot of stuff I didn't like, but I did like that." Another thing Chrys had noticed about her students—something she thought negatively impacted their writing ability—was that they had had no time devoted to "wandering and wondering" as children. All their free time had been spent in front of bleeping screens or in hyper-supervised organized activities. "I don't think kids do that much anymore."

"I know," Dee said. She leaned back against the side of her car, her hands in her pockets in an almost James Dean-ish pose. "When the fates conspired for me to move back here, I thought at least my daughter could have that."

"The fates conspired?"

Dee laughed. "That did sound a little dramatic, didn't it? What happened was, when my papaw died last year, he left his house and farmland to whichever of his grandkids wanted to live in it. Well, all the grandkids had grown up to live pretty urban lives, and nobody wanted it. I didn't even want it at first. But the deal was, if none of us wanted it, the place would be sold. And I couldn't stand the thought of that, especially because I knew what would happen if it got sold to the highest bidder…the house would be torn down, the trees cleared for lumber, the mountain blasted for coal. I couldn't live with that happening."

"And so you decided to move here?"

Dee broke eye contact for a moment and looked a little sheepish. "We decided to try it for a year. Anna was having some trouble with other kids in school, and I was still kind of recovering from getting divorced. I struck a deal with her that if she'd be willing to make the move, she could be homeschooled for the year. It just felt like time to try something different, you know?"

"So how do you like it?"

"Well, I love how beautiful it is," she said, waving in a gesture that took in the trees, the grass, and the surrounding mountains. "But I guess my answer would still have to be I don't know yet. We've not even been here for two months, and Anna won't start homeschooling till late August. How about you? You don't seem like someone who's spent her whole life in a holler."

Chrys struggled with how much to say. Dee seemed cool and sophisticated, but you could never really tell about people. "Well, I'm an English professor at a little college in Knoxville. I don't work in the summer, and Nanny was between caregivers, so I thought I'd help out for a little while." There. Nothing about her sexual orientation, the breakup, or her emotional crisis. Not the whole truth, but not a lie either. "I guess I felt like trying something different, too."

CHAPTER EIGHT

During the summer, Friday was always cookout night at Chrys's parents' house. When Chrys pulled into the driveway with Nanny in the Oldsmobile, Daddy was manning the grill, periodically setting down his spatula and trading it for a can of PBR. Chrys's mom and Dustin's wife Amber were carrying bowls of potato salad and Jell-O out to the big picnic table, and Peyton, dressed in a tiara and a pink bikini, was standing in the middle of a pack of Chihuahuas and Chihoundhounds and waving a plastic magic wand as if enchanting them to do her bidding.

Dustin opened the car door on the passenger side to help Nanny get out. "Sissy, I can't remember the last cookout you came to."

"I came to one a few years ago." Shit, how long had it been?

"You brung that lady doctor friend of yours," Nanny said. "I thought she was kindly stuck up."

Chrys and Dustin shared a smile. "Yeah, she was," Chrys said.

Meredith's trip to the cookout had been awkward. Chrys had felt like she was seeing the whole thing through Meredith's eyes: the cheap beer and Jell-O salads, the over-loud talk about hunting and NASCAR among the men, the rambling conversations about children and illness among the women, the Chihuahuas and hounds and their progeny and the landmines they left in the yard, one of which Meredith stepped in, soiling a two-hundred-dollar pair of running shoes.

The whole experience had been agonizing. Chrys wanted her family to approve of Meredith, but she had also wanted Meredith to approve of her family. All anyone had been able to manage was a kind of strained cordiality, and Meredith had commented later that it was symbolic that at "those kind of cookouts," the men claimed all the glory for the grilled entrees, while the women were relegated to the side dishes.

While Dustin got Nanny settled in a lawn chair, Chrys accepted a hug from Amber. "I'm sorry I ain't been up to see you yet," Amber said. "They had me scheduled a full shift every day this week, and by the time I got home and got supper fixed, I was just kilt." Amber was nearly twenty years younger than Dustin and pretty in an obvious, Hooters-girl kind of way: long strawberry-blond hair, big blue eyes, and a wardrobe to show off her youthful feminine attributes. Tonight's ensemble was an almost nonexistent peach-colored halter top and a pair of denim shorts that had been cut off so severely that there was hardly anything left of them.

"That's okay," Chrys said. "I've been busy getting settled in with Nanny." She didn't dislike Amber, but they certainly weren't close enough to necessitate Amber's apology for not coming to visit sooner. Except for a few jokes at Dustin's expense and some chitchat about Peyton, the two of them had little to say to each other, though that fact didn't stop Amber from talking.

"Hey, Chrystal!" Daddy hollered from his station at the grill. "Throw me that pack of weenies there on the table."

Chrys grabbed the hot dogs. It took some getting used to being called by her real name instead of the shortened form she'd used for decades. "Here you go, Daddy."

"They's drinks over in the cooler if you want one," he said, tearing open the hot dog package with his dentures. "Leaded or unleaded, whichever you want."

Amber was helping herself to a wine cooler, a beverage Chrys hadn't even known was still manufactured, though as long as there were guys who wanted to get teenaged girls drunk, she supposed the wine cooler would have a reason to exist. Chrys rifled through the cooler's sweating cans of Pepsi, Mountain Dew and Pabst Blue Ribbon. The women in the family generally didn't drink beer at social gatherings, but she didn't drink sugared soft drinks, and she'd be damned if she was going to stoop to sucking down a wine cooler just because she lacked a Y chromosome. PBR it was.

When Chrys took her beer into the kitchen, the first thing her mom said was, "Don't you want a plastic cup for that?"

"The can's fine."

Mom drew her lips together. "I don't care what you do. I was just thinking about Nanny. She don't say nothing about the boys drinking because she says men is fools anyway, but she might say something to you. She don't care for drinking."

"Then she shouldn't do it," Chrys said. "I, for one, am rather fond of it. Now is there anything else that needs to be carried out to the table?"

Once they were all seated at the picnic table, its yellow-checked plastic covering nearly obscured by containers of ketchup and mustard and pickles and chow-chow, Daddy passed a plate of meat and said, "Now these here is deer burgers." Sniffing the venison, the dogs circled the table in case either generosity or gravity might send some food their way.

"Tell Aunt Sissy what you call 'em, Peyton," Dustin said.

Peyton grinned, flashing a mouthful of baby teeth. "Bambi burgers!"

Chrys smiled squeamishly. It was a tough call whether to eat a hot dog made from God knows what or a burger made from a wide-eyed woodland creature. She finally decided to pass on meat entirely and made do with potato salad and fruit cocktail-studded green Jell-O, a meal she could've eaten just as easily had she been toothless.

"I remember one time we was eating deer mcat, and Chester broke a tooth on a piece of buckshot," Nanny said, swatting at a fly hovering over her potato salad.

"That ain't as funny as the one about him deer hunting early in the morning," Daddy said, around a mouthful of Bambi burger. "He fell asleep waiting on a deer to show up, and when he woke up a deer had peed on his foot."

Everybody laughed even though they'd heard the story before. It was one of the things families did.

* * *

After Nanny had retired for the evening, Chrys sprawled on her bed and called Aaron.

"Hey, honeybun. How are things at Green Acres?"

"Rustic. Tonight there was a cookout. We ate deerburgers and played cornhole."

"You played what?"

Chrys laughed. "Cornhole. It's a game."

"I'll make sure I tell that to the guys at the bar this evening."

"You're filthy, but I miss you."

"I miss you, too, honeybun. How's the heartbreak?"

Chrys's heart didn't feel broken so much as painfully hollowed out, as though somebody had gone after it with a melon baller. "I don't know. It's weird how you can build your life around somebody, and then they're just gone, you know? But not dead gone. Just gone away from you." She sighed. "But being here helps, I guess. At least I'm making myself useful. It's better than—what *is* that?"

Something was scratching at the window. She pulled back the curtain, fearing a wild animal or a maniac.

But the maniac in question was her brother, his idiotically grinning face framed by the window. "Aaron, my brother's at the, uh, window. I'll call you back, okay?"

She opened the window. "You scared the shit out of me!"

Dustin was holding three PBR tallboys suspended from the plastic rings that bound them. "Me and Amber wanted to see if you wanted to drink the last of the beer with us. I figured if I knocked on the door I'd wake Nanny."

"So you decided to make me pee myself instead?"

Dustin grinned. "It wouldn't be the first time. Remember when I stuck your hand in a bowl of warm water while you was sleeping and made you wet the bed?"

"I was twelve! You probably scarred me for life."

Dustin shrugged. "Yeah, so you gonna come out here and drink a beer with us or not?"

When Chrys stepped out on the porch, Amber was laughing. "You made her pee the bed?" she said.

"Yeah," Dustin said, pulling a can from its plastic ring and handing it to Amber. "But it ain't like she was always the victim. One time she put the deer-pee scent Daddy uses for hunting in my cologne bottle."

Chrys laughed. "Yeah, but you've got to understand," she said to Amber. "This is when he was in his heavy cologne phase in high school. The deer pee was a considerable improvement over what he usually wore."

Amber giggled. "I bet it was. High school boys stink no matter what. They either smell like too much cologne or like armpits."

Chrys refrained from commenting that Amber should know since she had been a high school student fairly recently. "Why don't we walk out into the yard so we don't wake Nanny?"

They settled at the round concrete picnic table in the side yard and drank their beers in silence for a few minutes. Finally Amber asked, "Are you sad cause you broke up with your... friend?"

"She don't want to talk about that," Dustin said.

"No, it's okay," Chrys said. "Yeah, I'm sad…especially since it was more of a *being dumped by* than a *breaking up with* kind of situation."

"The guy I was with before Dustin dumped me for another girl," Amber said. "I slashed his tires and smashed in the windshield of his truck."

"Wow," Chrys said, feeling both impressed and disturbed. "You hear that, Dustin? Don't cross her." Chrys was far too restrained and rational to slash the tires and smash the windshield of Meredith's Lexus, but she still knew that doing it would feel awesome.

"She's a firecracker," Dustin said. "It's 'cause she's a redhead."

Amber rolled her eyes. "Hey, us girls has got to stick up for ourselves. Right, Chrystal?"

"That's right." Chrys tapped her beer can against Amber's. "Hey, you were drinking wine coolers earlier. I didn't think you liked beer."

"I like beer better than wine coolers," Amber said. "I just can't handle the crap I get when I drink beer in front of your nanny. I don't think she gets that wine coolers have alcohol in them, too. And drinking beer in front of Peyton's even worse. She always says, 'Princesses don't drink beer, Mommy.'"

"I always knew there was a reason I never wanted to be a princess," Chrys said.

Dustin laughed. "Hey, what if all the Disney princesses did get drunk? That would be hilarious."

Chrys thought she detected a slight whiff of weed on Dustin's clothes, which would explain his flight of fancy. "Yeah, well, it'd be pretty hard to walk in glass slippers if you were shit-faced."

"Yeah, and like in 'Beauty and the Beast,' the beast wouldn't have to change into a prince," Dustin said. "Just give Belle a few beers, and he'd look fine the way he was."

"Beauty and the Beer Goggles," Chrys said.

They were laughing so hard they had to wipe away tears. It had been a long time since Chrys had had a good, long laugh with her brother.

When the laughter finally died down, Amber said, "That felt good. We don't laugh like we used to."

"Why not?" Chrys said. It was a nosy question, but it was out of her mouth before she could help herself.

"I don't know." Amber looked over at Dustin, then back at Chrys. "Money's been tight since Dustin lost his job, and in this part of the country the job offers ain't exactly pouring in."

"We ain't moving," Dustin said, his voice hard all of a sudden.

"I didn't say we was," Amber said, her voice hardening to match his. "I just said southeastern Kentucky ain't exactly the job capital of the world." She sighed and stretched out her legs, dragging her bare toes through the grass. "You know how it is. There's always something to worry about, and we just want to make sure we do right by Peyton."

Chrys nodded. "Sounds like you two have a bad case of grownup-itis."

"You've got that right," Dustin said, slamming his beer can on the table for emphasis. "Don't get me wrong. I love being a daddy. But a lot of being a grownup sucks. I remember when the hardest decision I had to make was whether to buy a cherry Popsicle or a grape one. Now I'm always having to decide something." He took a swig of PBR. "Hell, if it wasn't for getting drunk and getting laid, being a grownup wouldn't hardly be worth it."

Chrys found herself thinking of William Blake's *Songs of Innocence and Experience*, though she knew better than to discuss long-dead poets with Dustin. "But isn't there any time when you're with Peyton and she's so innocent and carefree you kind of get the feeling of being a kid again, too?"

"Sure," Dustin said. "And it's good while it lasts. But then I go to the mailbox, and there's another bill to pay."

"Speaking of bills to pay," Amber said, getting up from the picnic table. "I've got to work tomorrow."

"On Saturday? That sucks," Chrys said.

"Hey, people want to buy cheap crap on Saturdays, too," Amber said. "Bring Nanny by after she gets her hair done if she's up to it. We just got in some of that rose-scented soap she likes."

* * *

Nanny's beauty salon of choice, Klassy Kuts, was in a trailer on the outskirts of town. Nothing said classy like a hair salon in a trailer, Chrys thought. And spelling "classy" with a "k" really sealed the deal.

As soon as Chrys helped Nanny through the door, a heavily made-up, black-haired woman who looked like an aging country star said, "Well, look who it is!"

"You'd think I don't come here every Saturday of my life," Nanny muttered to Chrys before saying, "Hidy, Bernice. This here's my granddaughter Chrystal. She's staying with me this summer."

"Why, Chrystal, I bet you don't remember me fixing your hair for prom," Bernice said, her red, gooey lips spreading in a smile.

Chrys didn't at first, but then she was able to paint a picture in her mind by aging the woman backward. "Oh, you did, didn't you? You wove wildflowers into my hair."

"That's why I remembered it," Bernice said as she helped Nanny get settled in her chair and fastened a pink smock around her. "It was so different from what the other girls wanted back then. They was all about me making their hair as big as it would go."

Chrys had been the only girl at prom without an over-teased, over-permed mane. She had also been the only girl there with a gay boy for a date. "That was the eighties, all right," she said, without remarking that Bernice's hairstyle still seemed to be residing in that decade.

Bernice had Nanny leaned back in her chair and was spraying her thin hair. "Now who was it who took you to the prom, Chrystal?"

It was surreal talking about the prom as though it had happened yesterday. Apparently Bernice's hair wasn't the only thing about her stuck in the eighties. "Michael Brown. We lost touch, but I found him on Facebook recently."

"That's who I thought it was," Bernice said, working the shampoo into a lather. "He lives out in California and does something with computers. He came back here when his daddy died, and he had some feller with him he introduced as his husband. I thought they was gonna have to get a second casket for his mama, too."

Chrys felt like she'd just swallowed a handful of ice cubes. "Why is that?"

"Well, you know," Bernice said, sounding nervous. Apparently she had sensed the coldness in Chrys's voice. "People here just ain't used to things like that. I reckon it's a good thing you'uns didn't get married after the prom, huh? You would've been in for a surprise."

"No danger of that. We were just friends." She added "still are," even though her and Michael's only contact over the past two decades had been to friend one another on Facebook. She knew her defense of Michael had been feeble, but it was the best she could do when she was feeling assailed by homophobia herself and crushed under the weight of what Nanny didn't know about her.

Chrys spent the rest of Nanny's shampoo-and-set appointment pretending to be engrossed in a six-month-old issue of *Hair Today* magazine. When Nanny emerged from Bernice's ministrations, she had a cap of curls that reminded Chrys of a poodle in a dog show. "Is there anywhere else you'd like to go while we're out?" Chrys asked. "Amber said they just got in some of the soap you like at Dollar Tree."

"I do like that soap," Nanny said. "It smell likes real roses, not like some of them other soaps."

"The ones that smell like a chemist's idea of what a rose might smell like?" Chrys said. "We'll go get some, then. I had forgotten how much you love your bath things." She started the car and headed in the direction of Dollar Tree.

"We didn't have running water till I was sixteen years old," Nanny said. "And we didn't get a bath but once a week. Ma would get water from the well and heat it up on the coal stove and then pour it in a washtub. Us kids would take turns squatting in the washtub and using the lye soap she'd make every summer. That stuff would get you clean, but it smelled like bleach, and it left your skin as pink as a sunburned pig. The first time I had a real bath in a bathtub with hot running water I thought it felt better than anything else in the world."

"I bet it did," Chrys said.

"I always wonder about them people that says everything was better in the old days. I like my running water and my electric stove and my TV real good."

Chrys was driving through downtown, such as it was— Needham and Son Funeral Home, the Dixie Dog Diner advertising a two-for-one chili bun special, Miller's Florist, a law office and dark, empty storefronts that in Chrys's memory housed the Rexall drugstore and Newberry's five-and-dime. The streets were empty. "I bet you can remember when downtown was livelier on a Saturday," she said.

"Oh, law, yes," Nanny said. "There used to be a show here, and there was a soda fountain at the Rexall where I'd always get a chocolate milkshake. The stores stayed open late, and the streets was full of people. But that was before the mines closed."

Now most businesses were out near the Walmart by the interstate exit: a Sonic, a Jiffy Lube, a Huddle House, a Burger King. Chrys pulled into the parking lot of the Dollar Tree which occupied a spot in a sad little strip mall between a Little Caesar's and a tanning salon called Tanfastic.

"Hey, Nanny!" Amber called from her station behind the cash register as soon as they walked into the harshly lit store. "Chrystal, there's a wheelchair you'uns can use if she wants to look around."

As Chrys helped her into the wheelchair, Nanny said, "I always feel like a baby in a stroller in these things."

"Well, there are worse ways to feel, I guess." Chrys understood that Nanny didn't want to feel helpless. Still, it seemed like it might be pleasant to be pushed around every once in a while like a baby taking in the sights.

She wheeled Nanny through the aisles of off-brand, made-in-China crap: plastic toys that would no doubt break upon being removed from the packaging, figurines of ill-proportioned praying children, boxes of cereal with the same color scheme as the mainstream brands but with names like Oat Circles and Fruit Rings.

"Soap's up this aisle," Nanny said.

In the toiletries aisle was a sun-bronzed woman with wheat-colored hair pulled back in a braid. Something about the braid and the athletic body reminded Chrys of a picture of Artemis in the mythology book she'd repeatedly checked out of the library as a child. She felt a flip in her stomach she couldn't explain. But then the woman turned, smiled, and said, "Mrs. Simcox! Chrys!"

So the reason for the stomach flip had been recognition. The wheat-colored hair, the tanned, athletic body. Of course. "Hi, Dee," Chrys said.

"You ain't gonna make me get up out of this chair and stretch, are you?" Nanny said.

Dee laughed. "Nope. I'm off duty today, just hunting for bargains. Do you know there's a catalog that sells this brand of soap for twenty-four ninety-five a box? This is a deal."

"We came for soap, too," Chrys said. "Nanny likes the rose kind."

"Me, too," Dee said, "but the lavender's my favorite."

Chrys's mind sailed into a flight of fancy—what if there was a subtext to Dee's statement? Lavender—the soft, mysterious flower, color, and scent—was a code for lesbianism when it could not be spoken of openly. Idiot girl, Chrys chided herself. You're not exchanging coded flirtations with the likes of Natalie Barney and Renee Vivien on the Left Bank in the twenties. You're in a Dollar Tree in southeastern Kentucky talking to your nanny's physical therapist about soap.

"Lavender's nice," Chrys said stupidly as she grabbed three bars of the rose soap for Nanny.

"Here," Dee said, pressing a bar of the lavender into Chrys's hand. "Mrs. Simcox should try the lavender, too."

"Well, I ain't afraid to try something new," Nanny said.

Any thought that there had been a subtext to Dee's mention of lavender had just been eradicated. Either that, or Dee and Nanny were flirting with each other.

"Well, we'll see you Thursday," Chrys said, wheeling Nanny around a little too fast.

At the checkout counter, Amber said, "Are you all right, Chrystal? You look all flushed."

"Just a hot day, I guess," Chrys said.

"Well, it ain't hot in here," Amber said. She was wearing green eye shadow to match her green Dollar Tree shirt. "The manager keeps the AC cranked so high you could hang meat in here."

Once Chrys got Nanny in the car and slid into the driver's seat, a little smile sprung to her face. So she had a little crush. A futile crush, but a crush nonetheless. Futile though it was, a crush was still good news. It meant that even though Meredith had hurt her, she hadn't killed her.

"Look at you grinning like a possum," Nanny said. "What's got you so tickled?"

"Just glad to be alive."

"You think you're glad now—just wait till you're my age."

"Hey, I've got an idea." Chrys pulled out of their parking spot. She was getting better at maneuvering the giant Oldsmobile. "Let's go over to Sonic and get a big chocolate milkshake."

Now Nanny was grinning. "Law, I ain't had a milkshake in years."

Chrys patted Nanny's arm. "Well, that's a problem we can fix right now."

CHAPTER NINE

Going into the end of her second week staying with Nanny, Chrys had settled into a comfortable routine. She prepared simple meals, kept Nanny clean (a task which had gotten much easier thanks to the installation of a handicapped-friendly shower stall in the bathroom), and kept her company. She grocery shopped and picked up prescriptions at the Walmart pharmacy. Much to her relief, taking Nanny to church didn't fall into her range of duties. Her mom had showed up on Sunday morning, with Peyton in a frilly pink dress, to take Nanny to Piney Creek Free Will Baptist. "Now you're welcome to come with us," Mom had said to the still pajama-clad Chrys. "But I know you've got your own church in Knoxville that does things kinda different."

"Kinda different" was an understatement. On the dozen or so Sundays per year Chrys managed to get there, she attended the East Tennessee Unitarian Universalist Church, an institution that was about as different from the Free Will Baptist as two places calling themselves a church could be.

Chrys figured her mom and Nanny would be just as horrified by the UU flower communions and touchy-feely musings-disguised-as-sermons as she was by Baptist hellfire and brimstone. She was happy to let her mom tend to Nanny's spirit while she had the more comfortable duty of tending to Nanny's body.

Physical therapy was today, and Chrys was embarrassed to admit that she'd spent the past twenty-four hours anticipating Dee's visit. Never mind that Dee wasn't really coming to visit Chrys or to make any kind of social call at all. She knew she was being silly but figured that as long as she was aware of her own silliness, it was all right. When she found herself applying a touch of foundation and mascara before physical therapy time, she called herself a silly bitch.

When the knock came at the door, Chrys opened it to find Dee accompanied by a red hen that was pecking at her tennis shoes. "I don't know why," Dee said, "but this gal's been following me ever since I got out of my car."

Before Chrys could think of a witty reply, the hen sauntered into the house as if Chrys were her personal butler. Chrys leaned down to grab her and instantly remembered a farm fact she had forgotten: when chickens don't want to be caught, they're fast. The hen hung a quick right into the kitchen, her chickeny toenails clicking on the linoleum.

"Tinkerbell!" Nanny hollered from her recliner. "What in the sam hill are you doing in the house?"

"The chicken's name is Tinkerbell?" Dee asked, following Chrys into the kitchen.

"My niece named her," Chrys said, trying to sneak up on Tinkerbell, who stood, cocking her head quizzically, by the refrigerator. Once Chrys got in grabbing distance, the hen took off like a shot. Dee dove forward like a baseball player trying for a difficult catch, stretched out her arms, and nabbed Tinkerbell, who squawked in surprise.

"Okay, that was pretty amazing," Chrys said, laughing.

Dee pulled herself to standing, holding Tinkerbell under one arm like a football. "I've played a lot of softball. I never knew those skills would come in handy for chicken chasing, though."

Softball. She played softball and liked lavender. Chrys told her overactive brain to shut up. "Here, let me get the door so we can escort Tinkerbell out."

As Dee bent to put Tinkerbell down outside, she said, "Oh, shit!" and then "Excuse my language if you heard that, Mrs. Simcox."

Dee's exclamation had been quite literal. A splatter of chicken droppings decorated her forest green uniform shirt.

"I'm sorry," Chrys said. "I didn't know Tinkerbell intended to leave you with a parting gift. May I loan you a T-shirt?"

"Yes, please."

They returned to the living room to find Nanny wiping her eyes from laughing. "I swear, girls," she said. "That was funnier than anything I've seen on the TV in years."

Dee grinned. "The relief you get from physical therapy isn't usually comic relief." To Chrys's surprise, she pulled her soiled shirt off over her head and stripped down to her sports bra, revealing a tan, toned belly and more in the bosom department than her loose-fitting polo had implied.

"Uh, let me get you a T-shirt." She ran to her room, took three deep breaths to calm herself, and grabbed a baby blue shirt because it would complement Dee's eyes.

"Thanks," Dee said when Chrys held the shirt out to her. "I'll wash it and bring it back next week, okay?"

"Sure," Chrys said, unable to meet Dee's eyes to see if the baby blue complemented them or not. "I'll let you two get to work. Let me know if there are any more marauding chickens on the loose."

"Oh, I'll let Mrs. Simcox chase them. That can be our physical therapy for the day," Dee said, making Nanny smile.

In her room, Chrys paced, too full of nervous energy to sit down. She wandered over to the small bookcase in the corner, the only bookcase in the house. Chrys was the only voracious reader in her family. In the case were a small Bible, as opposed to the gigantic family Bible which sat on the coffee table in the living room, and a dictionary that probably dated from her mom's high school years. There were a couple of Billy Graham books, a copy of Johnny Cash's *The Man in Black*, and a dozen or so Westerns by Zane Grey and Louis L'Amour that had belonged to her grandfather. Snuggled next to *Riders of the Purple Sage* was a slim volume Chrys was pretty sure Nanny had never read: *Original Seine: Sensuality and Subversion Among the Women Writers of the Left Bank*. She shook her head at the academic-ese of the title. Why did so many academic writers feel the need to follow that pattern—a clever turn of phrase plus a colon plus a descriptive subtitle? When she'd first thought of the "original Seine" pun, she had been delighted by her cleverness. Looking at the book on the shelf, though, it seemed a much weaker title than, say, *Riders of the Purple Sage*.

She took her book off the shelf and sat down with it. The dedication read, "To Nanny, who taught me more than I ever learned in school." But the text of the book itself was probably incomprehensible to Nanny with all its theories and jargon and long quotations from difficult modernist texts. Reading it now, Chrys saw with a mixture of amusement and horror her much younger self: a wide-eyed novice academic who thought she was destined for a life of the mind—discussing ideas and developing theories, making significant contributions to her field. This freshly fledged PhD could never have predicted the low-level academic workhorse she'd become, teaching section after section of English comp to glassy-eyed freshmen who texted in class and couldn't sort out the correct usages of *their* and *there* to save their lives.

Squinting at her dense academic prose, Chrys questioned not only the reality of her current academic life but the dream of her imagined one. Was there really anything she could've said about Gertrude Stein or Djuna Barnes that hadn't been said at least a dozen times before? And who read these scholarly publications anyway? A few students probably skimmed them to lift out quotes for papers they were writing (the academic equivalent of strip mining). Some fellow academics might have read them, mainly to compare the "scholarly contributions" to their own. The scholarship that had been so exciting when Chrys was in grad school now seemed like a poorly attended circle jerk. She put the book back on the shelf.

When Nanny hollered, "We're done!" Chrys found herself stealing a glance at the mirror before going into the living room.

"I guess this is the part where I'm supposed to walk you out," Chrys said.

Dee smiled. "Wouldn't want me to get lost. Plus, you've got to protect me from the chickens."

Once they were out on the porch, Dee said, "She really likes having you here, you know."

Chrys couldn't help but feel touched and a little shy from the compliment. "I'm glad to hear that. I like being with her, too. Always have."

"There are some excellent paid caregivers," Dee said, leaning against the porch railing and looking out at the chickens pecking in the yard. "But when you're paid by the hour—and underpaid at that—you don't always go the extra mile to make sure the patient is happy." She turned around, and Chrys couldn't help noticing how the sunlight streaked her hair with gold. "It's not like having a granddaughter who'll take you out for a milkshake."

Chrys smiled. "The lady does love her milkshakes."

"I know taking her for a milkshake every once in a while seems like no big deal, but what you're doing is improving her quality of life."

"Now if I could just improve my own, that would be terrific." Chrys hadn't meant her joke to be revealing, but she could tell it was by the look on Dee's face.

"What do you mean?"

Now she'd done it. How to say something without saying too much? "Well, I guess you could say I'm in a transitional period in my life. I just got out of a long-term relationship... well, got kicked out of it, more accurately. And I don't know...I don't have what I want in life right now, but I don't exactly know what I want either. Is that what you call a midlife crisis?"

Dee was holding her gaze intently. "It's what I call *my* life crisis, or at least it's pretty close. I've been divorced for a year now. That's part of what brought me down here…the need for some distance. Well, that and my job in Cincinnati was taking up way too much of my time, and Anna was going through some stuff and really needed me. And then Papaw died, and here I am."

"When all else fails, move to Kentucky, huh?"

Dee laughed. "The destination of last resort. Hey, I've been talking to your nanny about Papaw's place—well, I guess it's my place now—and she says she'd like to see it. So I was wondering, maybe after her Saturday beauty shop appointment, you might stop by. I could make us some lunch."

Chrys felt herself looking everywhere but at Dee—at the chickens, the yard, the mountains in the distance—before saying, "I'd—I mean, we'd—like that."

* * *

After she heard snores coming from Nanny's room, she dialed Aaron. Somehow all the activities that took place after Nanny's bedtime—from reading in bed to drinking beer with her brother to calling Aaron—felt tinged with a teenaged naughtiness.

"How's the heartbreak, honeybun?" Aaron asked, as always.

"Still there, but I'm getting used to it. It's like growing a new limb or something."

"Yeah, but less useful. Having an extra arm would be the shit."

"Yeah. I do need to tell you, though…I think I might have a crush."

"Out in the boondocks? What do you have a crush on, a nanny goat?"

Chrys laughed. If a non-Southern urban person had made this joke, it would've pissed her off. But from the only black gay boy from Niota, Tennessee, it was funny. "It's neither a farm animal nor a relative, but thank you for asking. It's Nanny's physical therapist."

"You do like the healthcare providers, don't you?"

Chrys winced. "No comparisons between Meredith and Dee, please. Dee's totally different. Being a physical therapist, she's much more—"

"Hands on?" Aaron interrupted.

"Well, I don't know about that. Actually, I don't even know if she's gay. She's divorced, which could say straight."

"It could say gay just as easily. Be careful all the same, though. You put the moves on any local straight girls, and the peasants will be coming after you with torches and pitchforks."

"Don't worry. I managed to live here a lot of years without getting killed."

"But by God, if she is a dyke, fuck her ASAP. It's always a good idea to fuck a new person after a bad breakup. It washes the stink off."

Chrys muffled her laughter in her pillow so as not to wake Nanny.

* * *

Dee's family home was an old two-story farmhouse with gingerbread trim, much roomier than the tiny house where Nanny had raised her three children.

As soon as Chrys put her car in park, Dee bounded down the porch steps. "I'm glad you could make it," she said, opening the back door to get out Nanny's walker. "And Mrs. Simcox, my papaw's ramp is still in place, so getting up on the porch should be easy-breezy."

"It's a lovely house," Chrys said.

"I always thought so." Dee walked alongside Nanny. "Anna wants us to paint it purple, but I told her we have to wait till we've been here a year. Then if we decide we want to stay, we can paint it. There's no way I'm painting a house purple and then repainting it white so I can put it on the market."

"I don't know how you could move back to Ohio after living in a spot as pretty as this," Nanny said. She pronounced *Ohio* as *O-high*.

"Well, Ohio isn't all factories and smokestacks," Chrys said. "It has some pretty spots, too."

Chrys knew that Nanny and many Appalachians of her generation viewed Ohio as a vast industrial wasteland because so many of their male relatives had moved to smoke-belching Cincinnati or Dayton for factory jobs after the mines closed in the fifties. Apparently Dee was familiar with this stereotype of the state, too.

"It's a different kind of pretty, though," Dee said after Nanny had made it onto the porch. "I'd miss the mountains if I went back."

"I never could stand flat land," Nanny said. "There ain't no privacy and there ain't no place to hide."

Chrys laughed. "What have you got to hide from, Nanny?"

"You never know," Nanny responded cryptically.

"Here's the living room," Dee said once they were inside. "Decorated in thrift store chic, as you can see."

The couch was a vintage piece that had been reupholstered in purple. On the wall above it were shadowboxes displaying old thimbles, squares of quilts, and buttons. In the corner was a matching purple armchair with a tabby cat snoozing on it. A wooden sign with the word *Imagine* hung on the wall above.

"I like it," Chrys said.

"Me too," Nanny said. "It's different."

Dee laughed. "Well, I struck a compromise with Anna. We couldn't have a purple house, but we could have purple living room furniture. Want to look around the rest of the floor?"

Chrys almost gasped when they entered the next room. The walls were lined with bookcases full of leather-bound classics, paperback mysteries and contemporary novels. One corner of the room was occupied by a treadmill and a rack of weights. In the other corner was a squashy armchair occupied by a little girl with wheat-colored hair and red-framed glasses immersed in a copy of *Harry Potter and the Order of the Phoenix*.

Chrys felt a tug in her heart, remembering the solitary joys of a bookish childhood.

"Anna, could you step away from Hogwarts long enough to say hello to Mrs. Simcox and Ms. Chrys?"

Anna looked up, startled. "Oh…hello."

"Hidy, honey. That's a big old book you're reading," Nanny said.

"It's the fifth in the series," Anna said. Her feet were bare, and her tan legs were dotted with mosquito bites. Summertime legs. "They get longer and longer."

"You know, I must be the last person in the English-speaking world not to have read those." Chrys had been working on her dissertation when the Harry Potter craze first took off. She had been too buried in her scholarship to have time for popular fiction.

"Well, you've got to borrow one!" Anna said, as if she were dealing with a medical emergency. She sprang out of her chair and dashed for a nearby bookshelf. "Here's *Sorcerer's Stone*. When you finish it, I'll loan you *Chamber of Secrets*. The first two are super-fast reads."

"Thank you." Chrys probably wouldn't have been so generous with her books when she was a kid, but then, she hadn't owned many of them. "I'll take very good care of it."

"Nanny and Papaw used this room as a dining room," Dee said. "But I can only remember eating in it at Thanksgiving and Christmas. I guess we've always been eating-in-the-kitchen people."

"Our family, too," Chrys said. She thought of the dining room at Meredith's and how formal and fake it had felt sitting there, as though they were playing at being lord and lady of a manor.

Dee's kitchen was sunny, with red-and-white gingham curtains on the windows. The table and chairs were a vintage dinette set. "Oh, I remember these," Nanny said as Dee helped her to her seat. "You like old things, don't you?"

"I guess I do," Dee said.

"You reckon that's why you like me?" Nanny said, and they all laughed.

"I walked right into that one, didn't I, Mrs. Simcox?" Dee went to the fridge. "I made chicken salad for lunch, so you can have it on a sandwich or on some salad greens."

They ate chicken salad and drank lemonade, and Anna talked to Nanny about her love of craft projects. As soon as the dishes were cleared, Anna put a big plastic tub of beads and feathers on the table, and she and Nanny got to work stringing necklaces.

"If you're okay with Anna for a few minutes, I might take Chrys on a little walk around the property," Dee said.

Nanny grinned. "You go on. Me and Anna's fine here. We got necklaces to make."

When they were out of the room, Chrys said, "That looked like Nanny and me thirty years ago."

Dee smiled. "They both look happy. Anna can't really remember her grandma, so it's good for her to have a surrogate."

"It's good for Nanny, too," Chrys said as they walked down the front steps. "She has a great granddaughter, but Peyton's still a little squirmy when it comes to craft projects. She'd rather chase the chickens."

Dee grinned. "Well, as I'm sure you recall, I'm pretty good at that myself."

Out in the yard, they fell into an easy pace, walking side by side.

"This is the garden," Dee said as they approached a plowed field filled with neat rows of tomato plants, beans tied to poles, cucumbers and peppers. "This is about half of what Papaw put out, but this is just my practice garden. If we're still here next year, I'll do better."

"It looks good to me," Chrys said. "I remember when I was little I used to run through the garden rows, and when I saw a ripe tomato, I'd pull it off and eat it right then and there. The juice would be warm from the sun."

Dee ran over to a tomato plant, squatted, and plucked a ripe red fruit. She presented it to Chrys. "Knock yourself out."

Chrys paused for a second before accepting it, feeling a bit too much like Adam being offered the apple. But then, probably like Adam, she thought oh, what the hell, and bit into the warm red flesh. Juice ran down her chin. She laughed, and so did Dee.

"As good as you remember?" Dee asked.

"Absolutely. Here." She held out the tomato to Dee who leaned forward, lips parted, and took a big bite.

"Yum."

"I know, right?" Chrys imagined Dee leaning toward her not for a mouthful of tomato but for a kiss. Stop, she told herself. It's too soon, you're still too hurt, and this is nothing more than the middle-aged version of an unrequited schoolgirl crush. But even as she tried to reason with herself, she couldn't help noticing how red the tomato juice had made Dee's lips.

As they walked on, Dee said, "You know, I'm really glad I met you. I needed a friend here."

"Me too," said Chrys.

"And I wanted to say…if you ever need to talk, I mean, about your breakup and that kind of thing, feel free. I know when Anna's dad and I divorced, sometimes I just needed to vent."

"Thanks." Chrys knew she should say something else, but nothing else would come out.

"Of course, if you don't want to talk, that's cool, too. If I crossed a line—"

"You didn't at all," Chrys said. "But if we're going to be friends, I need to tell you that my breakup—my relationship— was with a woman. Is that okay?" She winced at her ineptitude. "I mean, I know it's okay…I've been okay with it for a long time. More than okay. But I mean, my being gay isn't a problem for you, is it?" There. The most awkward coming-out speech ever.

Dee's demeanor hadn't changed at all. "Of course it's not a problem. People like what they like. I've never understood why it's a problem for anybody."

"Me neither, but growing up here, it was a problem for plenty of people." On one level, Dee's response was reassuring: people like what they like, and it's not a moral issue. On another level, it was discouraging. It was the response of a straight girl…a nice, open-minded straight girl, but straight nonetheless. She thought of Dee's sensual smile as she held out the ripe tomato, then of the explosion of juice as she took a bite. As a feminist, Chrys had numerous problems with the story of Adam and Eve, but she had to admit it got one thing right: forbidden fruit was tempting.

CHAPTER TEN

"Hello?" Chrys was still in her pajamas, a cup of coffee in the hand that wasn't holding the phone.

"Chrystal, honey, I've got a splitter of a migraine, and I ain't gonna be able to take Nanny to church this morning." Her mom's voice sounded strained.

"That's okay. Just get some rest and feel better."

"I thought you'd pitch a fit."

"Because you have a migraine?" Really, did her mother think of her as that insensitive?

"No, on account of you having to take Nanny to church."

Chrys clearly needed more caffeine. Her brain wasn't firing on all cylinders. "I didn't say I'd take Nanny to church. I just said it was okay that you didn't."

"Listen, hon," Mom said. "Your nanny ain't never missed a Sunday of church unless she's been in the hospital, and even then she didn't think it was much of an excuse. Your daddy and brother's off fishing, and Amber's taking Peyton to that Methodist church over in Morgan. That just leaves you to take Nanny."

Chrys remembered all too well the hard pews of the Piney Creek Free Will Baptist Church and the even harder line taken by the preacher on the subject of sin. "Mom, this is the one thing I'm afraid I can't do."

"You know, when you was a little girl, I never heard you say 'I can't.' If somebody told you you couldn't do something, you'd try extra hard to do it, just to prove them wrong. I've prayed a lot on it, Chrystal, and I know you don't believe like your nanny does. I don't even believe all the way like she does. But I ain't asking you to believe. I'm just asking you to drive your nanny to church and wait in the parking lot till she's done. You can get one of the deacons to help her in and out of the building."

It had always been next to impossible to say no to her mom, and she knew church was the only place where Nanny got to socialize with ladies her own age. "Okay, but this isn't going to be regular thing."

"It'll be just this one time, I promise."

Nanny had three different "good dresses" she alternated between for church. Today it was the light blue one with the white eyelet jacket and white orthopedic sandals to match. Her hair freshly coiffed from yesterday's beauty shop visit, she smelled of rose soap and talcum powder. She draped her white purse over her forearm so she could hold onto her walker. "I'm sorry Joyce is feeling poorly, but I'm awful glad you're taking me," she said. "I ain't missed a Sunday unless I was in the hospital."

"I know," Chrys said. "Papaw used to say you were at church every time the door was open."

Nanny grinned as Chrys held the front door open for her. "And he never went but for Christmas and Easter and funerals. He always said, 'I married a virtuous woman so she'd do the churchgoing for both of us.'"

"I know you said your mama thought you were marrying a bad boy." She held Nanny's arm as they walked to the car.

"But he wasn't bad at heart," Nanny said. "He was a better man than he let on."

Once they were in the car, Chrys said, "You're gonna have to remind me how to get to this place. It's been a long time."

"I can't believe you'd forget as often as you used to go when you was little."

"I wasn't driving then."

Nanny laughed.

The Piney Grove Free Will Baptist Church looked just how Chrys remembered it: a plain white painted house with a small steeple and a hand-lettered sign. The parking lot was gravel, and once upon a time there had been two outhouses behind the church building. But when Chrys was ten years old, she, along with the other children at the church, had had the mortifying experience of going door to door selling candy bars to raise the money to buy the church an indoor toilet.

That wasn't the only memory that washed over her as she pulled into the parking lot full of pickup trucks and used Fords and Chevys. She could feel the itchiness of the dresses and the stiffness of the patent leather shoes she'd been forced to wear, could feel her belly rumbling in hunger as the preacher preached on and on. She remembered the love from Nanny and the other ladies in the congregation when they talked about how good and big and smart she was, but mostly she remembered fear. Fear as the preacher scolded them like disobedient children, describing how the flames of hell would make sinners' skin sizzle and pop.

There were also the fear-inducing questions raised by the stories: why did God test Abraham's faith by ordering him to kill his own child? Why did God torture Job in a way that seemed not only cruel but petty? And as she entered adolescence, the questions became more gender-based: why did Eve get all the blame for original sin? Why were women supposed to be subservient in the church and the home, and what was Paul's problem with the female gender anyway?

For each question Chrys had asked at home, Nanny had said, "You're smart, honey, but you can't outsmart the Lord. There's only one answer to your questions, and that answer's faith."

Chrys felt a light touch on her arm.

"Are you all right, child?"

She didn't know how long she had been sitting there in the parking lot without speaking or moving. "Yes. Just thinking."

Some members of the congregation were walking through the parking lot, men with their gray hair neatly parted, wearing Walmart dress shirts and dress pants, women in dowdy floral-print dresses and no makeup. They seemed like the exact same churchgoers from Chrys's childhood, frozen in time.

"I'm going to go get one of the deacons to help you get inside and settled," Chrys said.

Nanny looked surprised. "I thought you was gonna do it."

She supposed Nanny wouldn't find it funny if she said she feared being struck by lightning if she crossed the threshold. "Oh, I'm not going to the service. I brought a book. I thought I'd just sit under a tree and read until you're done."

Nanny's face clouded. "But this is your home church, honey. Looks like you'd at least want to visit it."

This was as bad as she'd feared. "Nanny, I've got my own church now in Knoxville."

"But you ain't in Knoxville today. Couldn't you just come in as my guest and let me show you off a little bit? You don't have to sing or shout or nothing, just watch."

Chrys sighed. Apparently she hated hurting Nanny even more than she hated setting foot in a fundamentalist church. "Okay, but this is the only time I'm going in."

The inside of the church was just as Chrys remembered: cheap paneling on the walls, a picture of the Last Supper with a WASP-y looking Jesus, and the horrifically hard pews.

A man with salt-and-pepper hair made a beeline for Nanny. He was afflicted with what Chrys thought of as "preacher puffiness"—an affliction peculiar to Baptist ministers who were not fat exactly, but somehow slightly inflated looking, perhaps from all the hot air the job required. "Mrs. Simcox!" he said, grinning. "We are so blessed to have you with us this beautiful Sunday morning. And this lovely young lady must be the granddaughter you've been telling us about."

"Yessir, Brother Higgins, this is Chrystal," Nanny said, clearly delighted by his attentions.

"Hello," Chrys said like a grumpy child being forced to make nice with a grownup.

"Your nanny tells me you're a schoolteacher over in Knoxville," the preacher said, shaking her hand in a death grip.

"I'm a college professor." She didn't mean to sound pretentious, but there was something about the word "schoolteacher" that called up images of ringing a bell outside a little red schoolhouse. To try to sound a little more down to earth, she added, "I teach English."

The preacher grinned and held up his hands in mock supplication. "Well, I reckon I'd better be careful how I talk in front of you!"

"It's okay. I'm off duty," Chrys said.

The preacher laughed far more uproariously than necessary, then strode off to greet another old lady.

As Chrys helped Nanny to her seat, Nanny spoke to a thin, bespectacled, sixty-ish woman holding a fat dumpling of a toddler. "This here's my granddaughter, Bella."

"She's adorable," Chrys said.

When she walked on, Nanny whispered in Chrys's ear, "She's had to take that baby to raise. Its mommy's on dope."

Chrys wondered if it was pills or meth, the two drugs that were epidemic in rural Appalachia and were causing many grandparents who'd thought they were done with three a.m. feedings and diaper changes to turn back the clock and do it all over again with their grandbabies. Chrys and Nanny found a spot to sit. It was so uncomfortable that Chrys couldn't imagine how miserable it must be for Nanny, but since when had Free Will Baptists been advocates of earthly comfort and pleasure?

The preacher stood and intoned, "We are blessed to be together in the presence of the Lord on this beautiful Sunday morning. Join me in singing 'Bringing in the Sheaves.'"

Just like in Chrys's childhood, there were no hymnals. Instead the preacher sang a line and the congregation sang it back to him. Chrys was shocked to find that she actually remembered most of the lyrics. When she was little she'd thought the hymn was called "Bringing in the Sheep" and had been disappointed to learn otherwise.

When the hymn was over, the preacher said, "I picked 'Bringing in the Sheaves' this morning because the Lord moved me to talk about the harvest, to talk about the reaping, to talk about where you'll be and what you'll be doing when them seven trumpets sounds and the Rapture is upon us!"

"Preach it," said a voice in the congregation.

Egged on, the preacher paced, more excited. "When the trumpets sounds, will you be righteous and ready? Or will you be popping open a Pabst Blue Ribbon? Will you be high on Jesus or high on pills? Will you be playing a harp or smoking a meth pipe?"

Chrys thought the last two questions must have been painful for the lady she'd just met. This was the first time she'd heard these particular drugs mentioned in a sermon, but with that exception, the preacher's words were as familiar as the fifth-rate Last Supper painting on the wall. It was all about either/or: alcoholism or temperance, depravity or chastity, sin or salvation, hell or heaven. There were no in-betweens.

It wasn't until she was a young adult that Chrys had been exposed to the fields of Christian thought and Biblical scholarship. The Free Will Baptists were opposed to seminaries and learned ministers, whom they dismissed as "educated fools." The only requirement to become a Free Will Baptist minister was the call to preach, and if some of the preachers Chrys heard growing up were any indication, literacy was not a prerequisite for the job. Once she had heard a young minister stumble over a Biblical passage several times before saying, "The Lord will help me through this word."

She had gotten so lost in her memories during the sermon that she was taken by surprise when the offering plate was passed her way. She didn't contribute, but Nanny put in an old, tissue-soft one-dollar bill. There was another hymn, and then the preacher announced the Lord's Supper. When the tray filled with tiny glasses of grape juice and oyster crackers was passed to her, she held it out to Nanny.

"You can take it, too," Nanny whispered. "You've been baptized."

She had been when she was twelve, in a muddy river where minnows nibbled at her ankles, not because she felt anything resembling a spiritual experience, but because it was what you did. She shook her head and passed the tray. Nanny placed the cracker on her tongue, then drank the juice, but her eyes looked sad.

In the car on the way home, Nanny said, "I feel foolish."

"Why?" Chrys asked.

"Because I thought if I could get you back in the church you'd realize you belong there."

"I don't belong in that church. I never have."

"Everybody belongs in God's house." There was a catch in Nanny's voice.

"Nanny, I love you and I don't want you to be upset, but that particular house of God has too many rules made by man. And you know I have my own church in Knoxville."

"I talked to the preacher about that place you go to. He said it ain't even a real church, that it's just a bunch of heathens."

Chrys smiled because it was kind of true—many Unitarian Universalists would happily embrace the heathen label. "Nanny, they're nice people who are open to a variety of beliefs. Do you honestly believe that Free Will Baptists are the only people in the world who are going to heaven? Or do you think heaven might be a little roomier than that?"

Nanny shook her head and smiled a little. "You've always asked the hardest questions. Even when you was a little girl."

Chrys's cell phone rang, and while she didn't always answer while driving, this time she was happy for the interruption. "Hello?"

"Hey." It was her mom.

"How are you feeling?"

"Well, I took one of them pills the doctor give me. So I'm high as a kite but I don't care that I've got a headache no more. Your daddy and brother brung some chicken from that place over by the lake if you want to come eat."

* * *

Chrys went into her parents' kitchen to find Mom and Amber setting out paper plates and plastic forks and her dad and brother and niece goofing off and getting underfoot. Chrys grinned at Daddy and Dustin. "So you went out to catch fish and came back with chicken?"

"That's right," Daddy said with a toothless grin in return. "The fish wasn't biting, but the chicken sure was."

Peyton giggled, and Dustin said, "I put a worm on my hook and felt a tug, and when I pulled it back, there was a chicken on the line, flapping its wings and hollering, 'Bawk! Bawk! Bawk!'"

"Liar," Peyton said, but she was still giggling.

"She ain't the first woman to call him that," Amber said in a joking-but-not-really tone.

"Come on, Sissy," Dustin said. "Keep me company while I smoke a cigarette."

Chrys sat on the glider while Daddy and Dustin smoked. They both held their cigarettes the exact same way, between thumb and forefinger. "I think Nanny's worried about my eternal soul," she said. "Why is it that you two can drink beer and skip church and she doesn't say anything to you, but when I do the same thing, it's awful?"

"It's 'cause your nanny don't expect men to have a lick of sense," Daddy said. "She thinks women ought to do better."

Dustin smiled. "I'm glad I'm a man then. It's easier to live up to low expectations."

"If your nanny knew the truth, she'd even think your mommy was a backslider," Daddy said.

"What was that?" Chrys's mom had poked her head out the door, probably to tell them it was time to eat.

"I was talking about what Nanny would think of that church you go to," Daddy said, grinding out his cigarette on the porch railing.

Mom looked embarrassed. "Your daddy's telling tales on me. Don't tell your nanny, but sometimes when she has another ride to church, I've taken to going to that new Fellowship church in town. It's that big building out by the interstate. It's real pretty on the inside—all modern, you know—and they don't care what you wear or how you look. Everything there— the music, the preacher—is just real happy and positive. All that hellfire and brimstone at the Free Will gets depressing."

"Tell me about it," Chrys said. So her mom was going to one of those nondenominational churches that seemed to be springing up everywhere—the kind that poured the old wine of Protestantism into new bottles of casual dress, praise music, and sermons with PowerPoint. "We'll add that to the list of things we don't tell Nanny."

"Yeah, speaking of them things," Daddy said. "How are you doing with your situation, punkin? You don't look as tore up as when you first got here."

Chrys felt a sudden sting of sadness, like always when she hadn't been thinking about the breakup but then was forced to. "I'm better. I think of her a lot but not all the time. And I'm sad sometimes but not all the time." She didn't add that she had recently discovered it was possible for her to have feelings for someone else, even if those feelings were fruitless.

Daddy nodded. "It's kinda like when I lost my arm. At first I felt like it was still there. Then after a while I knew it was gone and I spent a lot of time missing it. But then I got used to it."

"Yeah," Dustin said, "but losing an arm ain't all the way like losing a girlfriend 'cause you're never gonna think about your arm and say, 'I'm glad that damn thing is out of my life forever!'" He and Chrys and Daddy laughed.

Mom gave a huff and an eye roll and went back into the house, but Chrys was pretty sure she was hiding a smile.

CHAPTER ELEVEN

"Nanny don't get no good channels," Peyton whined.

"Doesn't get any," Chrys said. She did not presume to correct her adult relatives' grammar, but with Peyton she felt like she ought to at least expose the child to standard English.

"Doesn't get any," Peyton said in a clipped, Mary Poppins-ish British accent.

Nanny laughed. "Well, I reckon she put you in your place."

Amber had called early this morning, frantic because Peyton had run a low-grade fever the night before which was probably nothing but meant she couldn't go to daycare, and Dustin had already promised to cut some ladies' yards in town today, and they really needed the money.

Chrys was going to ask why Daddy couldn't watch her, but then she remembered one disastrous night from her childhood when Mom had been staying with a sick relative and had left Daddy in charge. Instead of running baths for them (why pay for all that hot water?), he had taken them out in the yard and sprayed them with a hose. Supper had been cold cereal which he accidentally served with buttermilk.

"Bring her over," Chrys had said.

Peyton was playing with the remote control, flipping rapidly back and forth between morning news shows as though doing so would make SpongeBob magically appear.

"You don't need to be watching that ole TV as pretty as it is outside," Nanny said. "You ought to out with your aunt Sissy and help her feed the chickens."

Chrys had a feeling the chickens wouldn't be too fond of this suggestion, but she said "Good idea!" anyway and grabbed a bucket of oatmeal and out-of-date milk she had stirred together for the hog.

Peyton followed Chrys outside, muttering, "Princesses don't feed no chickens."

"The princesses you like wouldn't have watched TV either. There wouldn't have been any. You never see Snow White watching SpongeBob, do you?"

Peyton giggled. "No."

"But some of those princesses might have kept chickens," Chrys said. "The eggs from the castle had to come from somewhere, and it isn't like Cinderella could take her pumpkin coach down to the Piggly Wiggly."

"You're so silly, Aunt Sissy."

Chrys thought of her recent actions in light of this statement: not seeing the infidelity that was happening or the breakup that was coming, healing a little only to get a pointless crush on a straight girl. "You're absolutely right, Peyton. Now don't chase the chickens before they've had their breakfast. You wouldn't like it if somebody started chasing you before you'd had your Pop-Tart in the morning."

"Are we feeding the chickens Pop-Tarts?" Peyton asked.

"Now who's the silly one?"

The chickens swarmed around them, clucking and tilting their heads quizzically. Chrys grabbed the sack of feed and let Peyton help her scatter handfuls. The chickens pecked and tossed their heads back to swallow, making pleased little chortling noises.

"They're saying 'om nom nom,'" Peyton said.

"They are, aren't they?" Chrys said. "You know what else they like to nom? Worms."

"Eew!" Peyton squealed.

It was fun spending time with her niece, living in the immediate the way one did in the company of children. That was one of the things she liked about kids—they were so engaged in their senses that they made you engaged, too. She was glad to become the kind of aunt who walked and talked with her niece instead of the kind who just stuck the occasional present in the mail.

As soon as they were in earshot of the pigpen, Porkchop started oinking up a storm.

"He's happy to see us," Peyton said.

"He's happy to get food. I don't think he cares who brings it."

The oinks turned into squeals as they got closer. Chrys dumped the bucket of slop into Porkchop's trough, and he fell to, slurping and snorting. Chrys turned to leave, but Peyton said, "Let's stay a minute and watch him eat. I think he's funny."

"He is a pretty noisy eater," Chrys said. "No one would compliment him on his table manners."

Peyton looked at Chrys, her eyes narrowed. "You don't like him, do you?"

She wasn't a stupid kid, Chrys thought. "It's not that I dislike him. I just don't let myself get to know him because I know what's going to happen to him."

"That's dumb," Peyton said. "He don't know what's gonna happen. It don't bother him, so why should it bother you?"

"I don't know. I think you're a better farm girl than I am."

Peyton picked up a stick and scratched Porkchop's back with it. "There you go, buddy," she said. He grunted, and his little eyes closed in ecstasy. "I ain't a farm girl. I'm a farm princess."

Walking back from the pigpen, Peyton said, "Can I play with the chickens now that they're done eating?"

Chrys remembered something she hadn't thought of in years. "Did your daddy ever show you how to hypnotize a chicken?"

"What's hippotyze?"

"Hypnotize. It's kind of like making somebody fall asleep except they're not all the way asleep."

"Like sleepwalking? I do that sometimes."

"Kind of. Come on. I'll show you." She took Peyton's hand, and they ran laughing toward the chicken coop.

When she and Dustin were kids, they thought hypnotizing chickens was the height of hilarity. Once a bird was under, you could move it to a random place, dress it in doll clothes, or nestle it in a catcher's mitt. After five minutes or so, the bird would snap out of it, act briefly disoriented, and then go about its business. As humor went, it certainly wasn't the height of sophistication, but even now, the memories made Chrys smile.

"Okay," Chrys said, surveying the selection of chickens. Roosters could be difficult, so she chose a little black hen. "Let's try it with this girl right here."

Peyton laughed. "That's Sleeping Beauty!"

"Well, that's perfect, then." Chrys knelt behind the hen and held her gently, pushing her head to the ground. With her other hand, she made a shushing gesture at Peyton. "Okay," she whispered. "This is what you do." She picked up a stick and drew a circle in the dirt surrounding the chicken. Then she drew a straight line extending from the chicken's beak to the edge of the circle. When she let go of the hen, it stayed still on the ground, staring fixedly at the line in front of it.

"She ain't moving!" Peyton said.

"She can't move. She's hypnotized."

Because Chrys had grown up in the land of country and gospel music, she'd had to play catch-up with rock 'n' roll once she left home. The first time she'd heard Iggy Pop's "Lust for Life" had been at a party in grad school where someone was playing the *Trainspotting* soundtrack. She had been immediately enthralled by the opening riff and Iggy's slurred snarl, and then when he sang the line comparing love to "hypnotizing chickens," she had laughed out loud.

A fellow partygoer who looked like he had answered casting call for English graduate student types said, "That is a delightful figure of speech, isn't it?"

Chrys answered that it wasn't just a figure of speech, that she had done it, and then proceeded to explain to a roomful of fascinated grad students the finer points of chicken hypnosis.

It was only now, with a broken heart which had mended just enough to stir again, that she truly saw the brilliance of Iggy's analogy. She watched the blissed-out, dazed hen, oblivious to all outside stimuli, seeming to look ahead while still unable to see what was right in front of her. It was a perfect metaphor for love.

After five minutes or so, the chicken started to snap out of it. She cocked her head a couple of times, shakily stood, and staggered drunkenly for a few steps before returning to chicken business as usual.

"So that's how you hypnotize a chicken," Chrys said.

Peyton applauded. "That was the best thing ever!"

"Better than SpongeBob?"

Peyton's brow creased in thought. "As good as SpongeBob."

"I can accept that."

Peyton slipped her hand back into Chrys's, and they began the walk back to the house.

"Aunt Sissy, look!" Peyton cried.

Chrys turned around, and there was the little black hen, following them like a puppy.

"She liked it," Peyton said. "She wants you to do it again!"

* * *

"Did she drive you crazy?" Amber asked when she came to pick up Peyton after work.

"No, we had a good day," Chrys said, tousling Peyton's hair. "She helped me feed the pig and chickens, and she helped

Nanny make a banana pudding. And she made some nice drawings to spruce up the refrigerator."

Amber smiled. "Well, you'uns is lifesavers. Hey, listen"— she looked around to make sure Nanny was nowhere in sight—"Me and Dustin's going out tonight. I'm supposed to sing over at the Tumbleweed Lounge. Your mama's staying with Peyton and said she'd be on call for Nanny if you wanted to come, too. I could pay you in beer for your babysitting."

"You don't have to pay me anything, but I'd love to hear you sing."

"I'm supposed to go on at nine, so we'll pick you up at eight, all right?"

After Amber and Peyton left, Chrys went into the living room where Nanny was watching the six o'clock news.

"Nothing but people on dope shooting each other," Nanny said. "I don't know why I even bother watching."

"No news is good news I guess," Chrys said. "Is it okay if I just fix us a quick supper tonight? Spaghetti or something?"

"That'd be fine," Nanny said. "I'm more tired than I am hungry. I love that young'un, but she wears me out."

"She is a ball of energy, isn't she?"

"Same as her daddy was at that age."

Nanny drank buttermilk with her spaghetti, which struck Chrys as disgusting, but the old lady drank buttermilk or coffee with just about everything. Chrys knew Nanny had had to do some adjusting to get used to her cooking; her go-to quick meals—spaghetti with jarred marinara sauce, omelets, big salads—were all dishes Nanny had politely described as "different." And they were different from the soup beans and cornbread and fried taters that Nanny had subsisted on all her life (though Chrys still made sure Nanny got her beans and taters at least once a week).

"Amber invited me to go hear her sing tonight," Chrys said, twirling her spaghetti on her fork. Nanny always cut her spaghetti into tiny, stick-like pieces.

"I don't reckon she's singing in a church."

"No, she's not."

"It's a shame to waste a pretty voice singing in a beer joint."

"Lots of great singers got their start in beer joints."

"Lots of great singers got their start in church, too," Nanny said.

Chrys had no choice but to agree with her.

* * *

The Tumbleweed Lounge was across the Tennessee state line. Amber was driving, as Dustin seemed to have gotten an early start on his beer drinking.

"I wonder why it's called the Tumbleweed Lounge," Chrys said. "It's not like there are any tumbleweeds in east Tennessee."

"Yeah, I never could figure out why people around here love western shit so much," Dustin said. "When you go inside, it's even worse. All these dudes wearing cowboy hats and boots, acting like they've been out riding the range or some shit when they've probably been blasting for coal or working at the Walmart all day. It don't make no sense."

"Maybe they figure a girl's more likely to go home with somebody who looks like a cowboy than a Walmart stock boy," Amber said.

Dustin laughed. "That's probably it. It's all about getting laid."

Amber laughed, too, but play-slapped Dustin. "I can't believe how awful you talk around your sister!"

"I'm used to it," Chrys said. "I grew up with him."

The parking lot of the Tumbleweed was full of pickup trucks festooned with NRA and "Friends of Coal" bumper stickers. Inside, it was dim and foggy with smoke, and Dustin hadn't been kidding about all the pseudo-cowboys. There were also a few biker types, burly and bearded, monopolizing the pool table. At the bar itself, a beer-bellied guy in a Kentucky Wildcats T-shirt was talking to a similarly built gentleman in a

T-shirt that read *God, Family, and Guns.* The few women were all in the company of men. They were also mostly bleached blondes who were decked out in a style Chrys's mother would refer to as "mutton dressed as lamb." Clearly, the Tumbleweed wasn't a popular choice for a girls' night out.

Dustin nudged Chrys. "What you drinking?"

"Well, a cabernet would be nice—"

"Don't be a wise ass. It's PBR tallboy night. You want one?"

"Sure. Thanks."

When Dustin disappeared to the bar, Amber said, "I hope this place ain't too nasty for you. I know you're used to better."

"Oh, I've been in worse," Chrys said, and it was true. Actually, if you changed the gender of everybody in the bar to female, the Tumbleweed wasn't that different from the dive bar she used to frequent in Lexington—right down to the patrons' western and biker attire. "I like a good dive bar. Always have."

When the three of them scooted into the vinyl, duct-taped booth with their beers, Amber said, "Don't worry, Chrystal. I'm just drinking one beer as liquid courage to get up there to sing. I'll be sober as a judge by the time we drive back."

Chrys popped open her tallboy. "Well, I'm glad to see my little brother had the good sense to marry somebody with some self-control."

Dustin grinned. "Why, Sissy, if I didn't know better, I'd think you was implying something about me." He lifted his beer can, took a long chug, and let out a voluminous belch.

"About you?" Chrys said, laughing. "You've always been a model of restraint."

"You know what's funny, though, Sissy?" Dustin said. "Compared to a bunch of guys I used to hang out with I might as well be a Baptist preacher. I mean, I've always like my beer and weed, but Tommy—you remember him from high school?"

Chrys nodded.

"He died from meth before he turned thirty-five."

Chrys pictured Tommy back when he was sixteen and hanging out in the now-unthinkable high school smoking area with Dustin. "That's awful."

"He had a couple of kids, too, but the state took them. And then Keith—my friend Jesse's younger brother—he OD'd on Oxy."

Amber nodded. "It's even worse with the younger people. Not that you'uns is that old."

"Thank you for that," Chrys said.

"But when I was in high school," Amber continued, "there was lots of kids scoring Oxy or crank. Scoring it or selling it."

"Why do you think the drug thing has gotten so much worse?" Chrys asked. She had been sober and studious in high school, and back then she had never heard of anybody doing much more than booze and pot.

Dustin shrugged. "Meaner times, meaner drugs."

"So many people feel so trapped with no chance of getting out of here and no future if they stay," Amber said, looking at Dustin, who looked away. "I guess the pills or the crank help them get away in their minds anyhow."

"Me, I'll stick to my beer and weed," Dustin said. "Course, Amber don't like me to smoke since Peyton was born."

"That's because it ain't legal, and I don't want nothing illegal going on with a child in the house," Amber said. "When it's legal, you can smoke it all damn day if you want to."

"They ought to make it legal," Dustin said, laughing. "It's the biggest damn cash crop in Kentucky."

Amber took a big gulp of beer. "Well, I reckon I'd better get up there."

"Do good, baby," Dustin said and kissed her cheek.

On the edge of the makeshift stage in the corner, Amber set a goldfish bowl with a sign reading "Tips." Her only accompaniment was canned music on an old boombox, which made Chrys wonder if this was going to be a painful experience. But when Amber sang her first note, all of Chrys's fears were erased. Amber's voice was as clear and bright as a mountain spring, with a little heart-tugging "cry" in it worthy of the queens of country music. Chrys hadn't listened to much country as an adult, so she didn't really know any of the songs Amber was covering, but she didn't need to know them to understand that Amber was singing the hell out of them.

Chrys and Dustin applauded wildly between each number, but weren't the only ones. Amber had attracted the attention of many of the bar patrons and had made unlikely fans of the bikers at the pool table.

"She's really good," Chrys yelled across the table.

"Ain't she?" Dustin said, grinning. "I'm gonna go on patrol for a minute and make sure none of these guys is thinking about hitting on her. I'll get us a couple more beers, too."

Chrys was almost halfway through her second tallboy when Amber launched into a song she actually knew, "Crazy." It took real courage to put one's own voice up against the great Patsy Cline's, but Amber, while no Patsy, still managed to capture the song's feelings of regret and longing. Chrys's eyes welled as she thought of Meredith when Amber sang "crazy for thinking that my love could hold you." God help me, Chrys thought as she blinked away her tears, I'm a country music cliché.

But then as Chrys continued to drink and listen, a transformation took place. When Amber sang the song's last drawn-out line, "crazy for loving you," the face that appeared in Chrys's mind was not Meredith's but Dee's.

"You crying into your beer, Sissy?" Dustin asked.

"Maybe a little. It's a beautiful song."

"Willie Nelson wrote it, you know," Dustin said. "Speaking of fellers who like to smoke weed."

When Amber announced a short break, Chrys excused herself for the ladies' room. She did so with some trepidation—she knew the room was about as likely to be clean as it was to contain actual ladies—but after two tallboys, her bladder was sloshing.

The restroom was as dank and foul as she'd imagined, and emerging from her stall, she discovered that her neighbor in the adjoining one had been Amber, who was now trying to look in the smeared, fly-specked mirror to fix her lipstick. "Oh, hi!" she said. "Them last two songs, I had to pee so bad I thought I was gonna die."

Chrys turned on the tap and made a gesture of washing her hands, though there were no soap and no towels. "You're really good, you know. What you need is a kick-ass band to back you up."

"I know, right?" Amber said. "So you think I'm, like, professional-quality good?"

"I'm no expert, but I can totally imagine hearing your voice on the radio."

Amber flashed a little-girl smile that was just like Peyton's. "Thank you. That means a lot." She patted Chrys's arm. "Listen, I've been wondering if you might be willing to talk to Dustin for me. He really looks up to you, you know."

"What about?" Chrys cut Amber off before she could butter her up any more.

Amber looked around as though spies were everywhere. "I've been trying to talk Dustin into moving to Nashville so I can have a chance at being discovered. I know there's lots of people with the same dream, but here my chances is zero. The thing is, Dustin would have a better chance there, too. His unemployment's fixing to run out, and there ain't no jobs around here."

"There would be more jobs in Nashville," Chrys said.

"And you know what?" Amber said. "Dollar Tree's a chain, and there's six of them in Nashville. I've already gotten approved to transfer to a store there."

"You've really done your homework, haven't you?"

Amber nodded, her eyes shining. "It'd be good for Peyton, too. Good schools, after-school activities—"

Chrys recognized Amber's longing because she had once felt something similar herself. "Dustin is totally against this?"

"So far. It's like he laughs it off, like we couldn't really do it. To be honest, I think he's scared."

"He probably is. He's taken a lot of silly risks in his life, but he's never taken a serious one. You want me to talk to him?"

Amber took both of Chrys's hands in hers. "That'd be great. Not tonight, though. Sometime when he's sober and will actually listen to you."

"Okay." Chrys hesitated a moment, then decided to ask the question that was on her mind. "So like I said, I think you've got the talent to succeed. But there are lots of people with talent who never make it. What are you going to do if you go to Nashville and things don't happen for you?"

Amber's expression was defiant. "Well, I'll tell you what I'm not gonna do. I'm not gonna come back here with my tail between my legs and work at the Dollar Tree for the rest of my life. If the music thing don't happen, I want to go back to school. I want to make something of myself so Peyton will be proud of me and want to make something of herself, too."

"Okay," Chrys said, relieved that Amber was no fool with stars in her eyes—she had a backup plan. "I'll talk to Dustin… when he's sober."

To Chrys's surprise, Amber threw her arms around her. "Thank you so much."

"I'm happy to do it." Chrys looked around at the filthy bathroom where they had been standing for entirely too long. "You know, this is the nastiest place I've ever had a serious conversation."

"Me too," Amber said, laughing.

When they returned to the table, Dustin said, "I thought you'uns had drowned in there."

"Nope," Amber said and gave him a peck on the cheek. "I'd better get back up there and sing."

Dustin shoved a fresh can of PBR toward Chrys. "Just what I need," Chrys said. "Now I'll go from tipsy to shit-faced."

"Nothin' wrong with that," Dustin said. "I'm outdrinking you two to one, so I'm already there."

Chrys popped open the can. "I'm going to feel like a teenager, sneaking into Nanny's house drunk."

"You're gonna feel like me as a teenager, you mean," Dustin said. "You was always home hitting the books."

When Amber took the stage, she said, "I'd like to dedicate this next song to Chrystal."

"Shoot," Dustin said, grinning, "what was you two doing in that bathroom anyway?"

"You're awful," Chrys said, laughing. Fortunately, the song Amber sang was about friendship, not romance.

After Amber's set ended, she came back to the table flushed and seeming to buzz with adrenaline. "Chrystal, you care if Dustin and me put some money in the jukebox and dance to a couple of songs before we go? I've got to get rid of some of this nervous energy."

"I know another way to get rid of it," Dustin said, leering.

"Well, we'll see if you're up for it, drunk as you are," Amber said, laughing.

He put his arm around her. "You know I'm always up for it."

"TMI, you two." Chrys waved them off. "Go dance."

Sitting alone, Chrys realized how drunk she was. It was a heavy, bloated, burpy kind of drunk, not the light, loose feeling she got from wine. Watching Dustin and Amber dance, laughing and in love, her fuzzy, buzzy brain wandered back to Dee. In the past when she'd had a crush and then discovered the woman was straight, her romantic feelings had always turned off like a faucet. Why not this time? Was it because she was on the rebound? Was it because she was indulging in masochistic behavior? Or was it that ultimate lesbian fantasy come true, that the straight girl she wanted wasn't really straight at all?

Recognizing that she had been robbed of her judgment even as she did it, she took out her phone. It was too late to call; plus, she knew she'd sound drunk, so she opted for a text: *Hi, it's Chrys. I owe you lunch. Nanny has a doctor's appointment at the hospital on Wednesday. Do you want to go somewhere then?*

Unlike her young students, whose fingers were incredibly dextrous on phone keys, Chrys was a painfully slow texter. Part of it was probably a generational thing, but a lot of it was her insistence on standard capitalization, punctuation and spelling.

Almost immediately after she hit send, a reply came back: *Sure, the Mexican place across the street from the hospital is pretty good.*

When Amber returned from dancing, she said, "What are you grinning at?"

Chrys felt her face heat up. "Nothing. Just a text from a friend."

CHAPTER TWELVE

"Are you sure you're okay with me going to lunch while you have your doctor's appointment?" Chrys asked as she pulled into the hospital parking lot.

"I done told you it's fine. Just help me into the office."

Nanny had said she had an appointment to see a lady doctor, so Chrys was confused when the name on the door read Dr. Gary Carter. But when she helped Nanny into the waiting room of female patients, some of them pregnant, she understood that Nanny had meant not a lady doctor, but a doctor who treated lady parts. After Chrys got Nanny seated with a not-too-ancient issue of *Good Housekeeping*, she went to speak to the heavily made-up woman at the check-in desk. "I'm dropping off Mrs. Simcox. If I write down my cell number, will you call me when she's ready to be picked up?"

"I sure will, sweetheart. We'll take good care of her for you."

El Toro, the Mexican restaurant across the street from the hospital, was decorated in standard sombrero-and-serape motif. Dee was already waiting for her at a corner table. Even in her work uniform, she was lovely. Chrys's stomach felt like it was full of Mexican jumping beans.

"Hey," Dee said, "did you get your nanny settled?"

"I did." Chrys slid into the booth. She told Dee about the "lady doctor" confusion, and Dee laughed.

"I ordered us some guacamole," Dee said. "I didn't know what you'd want to drink."

"Well, what I want is a margarita, but I guess that's out of the question."

Dee smiled. "There is something tragic about a Mexican restaurant being in a dry county. But I'm still thankful this place is here. The thing I miss most about the city is the diversity of the food. Sometimes I'd kill for a piece of sushi."

"Yeah, well, I wouldn't hold my breath for sushi to come to southeastern Kentucky any time soon." The waiter arrived with the guacamole, and Chrys ordered iced tea. "I miss the food in Knoxville, too, but I have to say it's been interesting revisiting the food of my childhood. I swore off beans and cornbread as a teenager, but now I'm back on them again."

"Fallen off the wagon, huh?" Dee dragged a chip through the guacamole. "So it's been good for you so far, coming back for the summer?"

"It has. I've been grateful for getting to spend time with Nanny, and it's forced me to focus on something other than my own problems. But some stuff is weird, too. Going to church with Nanny is an experience I won't repeat if I can help it."

Dee nodded. "All the churches here are so conservative. It's like the most radical, left-wing thing you can be is a Methodist. I'd been taking Anna to a Quaker church in Cincinnati, but we haven't been going anywhere here because there's nothing that's liberal enough."

"Yeah, well, I'm a Unitarian, so I'm definitely out of luck in these parts."

Dee laughed. "Wow, you really are a heathen, aren't you?"

After the waiter took their orders, Dee said, "You know something that confuses the hell out of me about this part of the country? All the dirt-poor Republicans. I see all these patients who are barely scraping by on government assistance, but on their beater cars they have bumper stickers supporting the very candidates who want to do away with the funding they live on."

"My daddy's that way," Chrys said. "He lives on disability and votes for politicians who rant about people sucking off the government, never thinking he's one of those suckers."

"I'm glad I have you to talk to," Dee said. "I don't know what I'm going to do when you leave at the end of the summer."

"Me neither," Chrys said, feeling the truth of her words. She didn't know what she was going to do, period.

"You know," Dee said, "when you and Nanny came to my house, I could tell you were surprised by how many books I had."

The waiter arrived with their lunch, and Chrys was grateful for the interruption since it allowed her to collect her thoughts. "Well, I knew you were smart. I just didn't know how much of a reader you were."

"I'll tell you a secret," Dee said. "I was an undergraduate English major just because I loved to read. After I graduated, I worked in a bookstore for a year and then started applying to grad schools. I got into a couple but not with any money. My dad, who's a really practical man, had a talk with me about whether or not it was sensible to go into major debt for an advanced English degree. I decided it wasn't."

"So why physical therapy?" Chrys cut into her chimichanga.

"My mom had gotten hurt in a car wreck. It was so bad she couldn't walk for a while, and physical therapy really helped her. I figured the world probably needed another physical therapist more than it needed another professor rattling on about Jane Austen. No offense."

"None taken. But with the students I teach, I usually rattle on about things like how to write a decent paragraph."

"Well, that's useful," Dee said. "That helps people."

"You think so?" Chrys was a little surprised. "It's not exactly teaching the lame to walk."

"But it's helping people think, which for a lot of people comes a lot less naturally than walking."

"True." A crazy idea flashed into Chrys's head. "Hey, I just thought of something. Last night my friend Aaron called to remind me that the production of *A Midsummer Night's Dream* that he's in opens in Knoxville this weekend. Mom's going to look after Nanny, and I'm going to go see it Saturday night, spend the night at Aaron's, and drive back Sunday morning. Do you want to come with me? We could have sushi before the show."

Dee's grin looked a little incredulous. "You're inviting me on a road trip? Why?"

"Because I like you." Despite her casual tone, Chrys was nervously wadding her napkin under the table.

"I like you, too." Was it Chrys's imagination, or did Dee hold eye contact with her a little longer than necessary? "Well, I'd have to see if Anna can spend the night at her friend's house, but she's over there most Saturday nights, so it shouldn't be a problem."

"So that's a tentative yes?"

"Yes. Or yes, tentatively."

Chrys had to try very hard not to sound as excited as she really was. "Great. I just thought that being a city girl, you might like getting away to a marginally more urbane environment for a few hours." Stop babbling, she told herself.

"It's funny," Dee said. "I'm a city girl but at the same time I'm not. I grew up in the city, but my parents always lived as transplanted hillbillies, and most of their friends were transplanted hillbillies, too. I probably ate beans and cornbread just as much as you did." A sly smile crossed her face. "I noticed that your nanny calls you Chrystal."

"I dropped the second syllable when I went to college. I thought Chrystal sounded like a name country people would come up with when they wanted to sound fancy."

"Loretta Lynn has a sister named Crystal, doesn't she?"

"Yeah. Different spelling, though."

"Well, in case you don't think I have country girl credentials, I'll have you know I dropped a couple of syllables from my name, too."

Chrys laughed. "Really? What was it?"

"Oh, I don't think I'm going to tell you yet. I think I want to remain a woman of mystery for a little while longer."

"If I guess it right, will you tell me?"

Dee's face lit up when she laughed. "Sure, but if you got it right, I'd probably faint from the shock. It's one you don't hear often. And at least Chrystal sounds pretty—my name doesn't. It's something I share with only my closest friends. Well, and people who have to look at my driver's license." She glanced at her watch and said, "Ooh, I've got an appointment in twenty minutes. I'd better scoot."

Chrys paid the bill, and they walked outside together and stood—a little awkwardly, Chrys thought—in the parking lot.

"Thanks for lunch," Dee said, and to Chrys's surprise, she stretched out her arms for a hug.

It was a real hug, close and warm, not one of those half-assed lean-over-and-pat-each-other's-backs deals. Chrys felt the strength in Dee's arms and didn't want to let go, but she knew that social cues dictated a time limit on public, parking-lot hugs between friends.

In the car, waiting to pick up Nanny, Chrys imagined she could still feel the warmth of Dee's touch. She wondered if she was imagining other things, too—for instance, that the lunch conversation had sometimes verged on the flirtatious. But there was one thing she didn't have to wonder about. Dee had said yes to the impromptu invitation to dinner and a play. She hadn't hemmed or hawed or made an excuse or said yes on the condition that it was not a date. She had just said yes. And a yes from Dee—even if Chrys wasn't one hundred percent sure what it was a yes to—felt great.

On the way from the hospital, Nanny said, "Can we stop where that feller's selling produce off his truck? He had a sign saying he had some white half runners."

"Sure," Chrys said.

"I'm wanting a summer supper tonight—some of them beans cooked with taters, corn on the cob—Silver Queen if he's got it—and some slicing tomatoes."

"Sounds good to me." Chrys pulled off at the side of the road where an old man in overalls stood next to an old Chevy truck, both of them seemingly frozen in time. In the bed of the truck were bushel baskets of produce: green beans, yellow squash, corn, tomatoes. "It looks like we're in luck," Chrys said.

"Well, don't let him be stingy with the beans. Make sure you get a nice mess," Nanny said.

"Yes, ma'am." Chrys got out of the car.

The old man grabbed the straps on his overalls and said "Hot enough for ya?" and Chrys replied that indeed it was. She chose what she hoped was a good amount of white half runners, three tomatoes and four ears of Silver Queen corn. When she got back to the car, she showed Nanny the bag of beans. "Did I do okay? He didn't stiff me, did he?"

Nanny nodded her approval. "No, you done good. That's a nice mess."

Chrys had asked Nanny the question in part just to hear the phrase "a nice mess" again. She liked how oxymoronic it was—a mess was by definition imprecise and chaotic, but putting "nice" in front of it somehow implied embracing this state. Maybe that's what Chrys was doing. Trying to turn her life from a mess into a nice mess.

* * *

Chrys and Nanny sat on the porch swing, a pot between them, breaking beans. It was peaceful, concentrating on nothing more complex than pulling the strings from the pods, working in companionable silence.

"This is nice," Chrys said after a while.

"It is." Nanny's hands were swollen and stiffened from arthritis, but she was still an efficient bean stringer. "I always did like breaking beans, shucking corn. That wife of your brother's had never broke a bean till I showed her how. She'd never eat a vegetable growing up unless it came from a can."

"That's sad." It had been a long time since Chrys had broken beans herself, but she found herself getting the knack again. She had forgotten how much she liked the clean, earthy smell of a freshly snapped green bean.

"I know it. A canned green bean don't taste like nothing but the inside of the can. Amber's a good girl, but she grew up in a sorry family. I think part of the reason she married Dustin was to get away from them."

"You know, I don't think many of the kids I teach have had much exposure to real food preparation either. Sometimes one of them will write a paper about a family recipe, and it'll be something like Kraft macaroni and cheese mixed with a can of tuna."

"Law, that's just nasty," Nanny said, grimacing. "You might as well eat cat food."

"I know," Chrys said, laughing. The phone rang from inside the house, and she excused herself to answer it.

"Hey," her mom said. "We got a big mess of white half runners and some corn and maters if you want to come eat this evening."

Chrys laughed. "Did you by any chance buy your produce from an old man in overalls out by the Gas 'n' Go?"

"The beans and corn we did, but the maters is from your daddy's garden."

"Nanny and I bought the same stuff from the same guy on the way back from her doctor's appointment. We were just sitting on the porch breaking beans."

Her mom whooped with laughter. "Well, why don't you bring your mess over and we'll put our messes together?"

"Sounds like what families do," Chrys said. "As long as Nanny's up for it, we'll be there."

* * *

After supper, Chrys and her mom and Amber worked on the dishes while Nanny sat at the table with a cup of coffee.

"I feel sorry as bluejohn just sitting here," Nanny said. "I wish you'uns would give me a job to do."

"You're keeping us company," Chrys's mom said, washing a plate which she passed to Amber to rinse. "That's your job."

"What amazes me is that men don't offer to help with the dishes." Chrys took the plate from Amber and wiped it with a dishtowel.

"Well, then you're gonna spend your whole life being amazed because they ain't never gonna help," Amber said, and they all laughed.

"Well, your daddy says he can't help with the dishes on accounta just having one arm," Chrys's mom said. "Before he lost that arm I don't remember what his excuse was."

"Joyce, that's awful," Nanny said, but then the corners of her mouth twitched and she was laughing and so was everybody else.

"Well, men have their uses," Amber said. "Dustin killed a spider for me in the bathtub the other day."

"Well, the Lord gave men and women different gifts," Nanny said.

"And the man shalt smite the spider while the woman shalt wash the dish," Chrys said, drying the last plate. It was funny; a roomful of straight Appalachian women could be harder on men than a roomful of lesbians.

"I love you, honey, but you are some kind of backslid," Nanny said.

Chrys kissed the top of Nanny's head. "I know it. And I love you, too."

"Hey, Chrystal, I need to go outside and check on Peyton," Amber said. "You wanna come with me?"

"Sure." It seemed a transparent ruse for a private conversation, but Chrys went along.

As soon as they were out of the kitchen, Amber whispered, "I got approved for that transfer to Nashville. I can start in October if Dustin'll go."

"Okay. I can talk to him tonight if I can get him alone."

"I'll try to make that happen," Amber said.

Chrys couldn't help grinning to herself. Were heterosexual relationships always so full of maneuvering and subterfuge?

Chrys's dad and Dustin were on the porch, smoking. Peyton was in the yard, blowing soap bubbles at which one of the Chihoundhounds snapped aggressively.

"Me and your brother was just talking politics," Daddy said. "I was telling him he needs to get out and vote in November."

"And I was telling him it don't matter who you vote for, they're all bought and sold anyway."

Chrys smiled. "What was it Gore Vidal said? 'By the time a man gets to be Presidential material, he's been bought ten times over.' What I don't agree with Daddy about is who the lesser of those two evils would be."

"Well, I ain't voting for anybody who's gonna take away my guns," Daddy said.

Chrys suppressed an eye roll. "Daddy, the guns you have are for hunting deer, and nobody wants to take those away from you."

"They might not be just for deer," Daddy said. "If somebody was prowling around this house of a night, I'd shoot 'em and drag 'em into the house before I called the law."

"I'll bear that in mind the next time Nanny sends me down here in the middle of the night because she's out of Pepto-Bismol," Chrys said.

"Hey, Dustin," Amber said, like she'd been waiting a while to get a word in, "would you run over to the trailer and get those new pictures of Peyton for your mother and daddy? Chrystal, you can go, too, and see that…that thing I was telling you about."

"Okay," Chrys said, though she was sure Dustin knew he was being set up.

When Chrys and Dustin walked past Peyton, she said, "If you're going to the house, bring me a Popsicle."

"What does Barney say the magic word is?" Dustin said.

"Please!"

"I can't believe my badass brother just quoted Barney the dinosaur," Chrys said.

Dustin shrugged. "Hey, whatever it takes. If a purple dinosaur tells her to do something, she's more likely to do it than if I tell her."

Dustin had bought the used trailer cheap through a classified ad in the local paper, and while it was in good condition, it showed its age. For one thing, unlike more contemporary trailers, it wasn't built to resemble a house on the outside. It was metal, flat-roofed, and as rectangular as if it had been connected to the cab of an 18-wheeler. On the inside its age showed through stylistic elements—the dark, fake wood paneling, the kitchen cabinets with simulated carved details and ornate brass handles—all clearly set the time of the trailer's manufacture sometime in the early eighties. Amber had obviously tried to give the place her own touch, with pictures of Peyton and a couple of those Anne Geddes prints of babies sleeping in big fake flowers, but the look of the trailer was so dated it made Amber's efforts seem anachronistic. The paneled walls cried out for a macrame owl.

"What was it you was wanting to see?" Dustin asked.

Chrys saw no reason to keep up a ruse that had been so half-assed in the first place. "Nothing. I promised Amber I'd try to talk to you."

Dustin shook his head, half-grinning. "Well, I walked right into this one, didn't I?"

"Yep. Railroaded by devious women."

"The story of my life. Well, we might as well sit down."

Chrys sat down next to Dustin on an old couch Amber had disguised with a blue and white checked slipcover.

"This is about Amber wanting to move, ain't it?"

"What are you, some kind of a mind reader?"

"Don't have to be a mind reader the way she's been dropping hints." Dustin shook a Marlboro out of the pack and lit it.

"She really wants this chance, Dustin. And she's talented enough that she just might make it. Being young and pretty won't hurt either."

Dustin squinted through his cigarette smoke. "All my life I've heard people talking about how they was gonna get out of this place and do wonders and shit thunders. Do you know how many of them actually did what they said they was gonna do?"

Chrys shook her head.

"One. And that was you. The rest of them was all talk and never made it over the county line. Or else they went off for a while but then come back home on the bus, flat broke."

Chrys knew there were lots more people than her who had gone on to succeed outside the area, but she also knew Dustin was utterly convinced by his own anecdotal evidence. "Well, at least they tried."

"They tried and they failed," Dustin said. "But you know what? If you never try, you never fail. That even worked for me in high school. I never tried, but they passed me along anyway, and I ended up getting the same high school diploma you busted your ass for."

"Sad but true," Chrys said. "I understand that you've always kept your expectations and responsibilities low, Dustin. But how low are you willing to go? Your unemployment's going to run out soon, and what kind of job opportunities are you going to have around here? Stocking shelves at Walmart for minimum wage and no benefits?"

"You think Nashville'd be better? Things is bad all over, Sissy."

"I know, but a big city does mean more jobs and more opportunities. There'd be opportunities for Peyton there, too. Good schools, extracurricular activities—"

"And drugs and gangs and violence. A big city means more bad people. I can't take Peyton away from her home and her grandparents. Here I know I can keep her safe."

It never failed to amaze Chrys how hard people clung to the illusion of safety. "What, and there aren't bad people and drugs here, too? Weren't you telling me the other night at the bar about how many friends you'd lost to meth or Oxy? This place isn't safe either; it's just familiar. I don't think you're scared for Peyton, Dustin. I think you're scared for yourself."

"All right." Dustin stood up. "I reckon you can tell Amber you gave me my talking-to. I'm gonna get Peyton a Popsicle."

Chrys got up, too. As they left the trailer, she said, "Remember Amber wanted you to bring those pictures."

Dustin shut the door behind him. "She can get them herself."

CHAPTER THIRTEEN

Chrys had worried that the ride to Knoxville might be full of awkward conversational gaps. But she and Dee had immediately fallen into comfortable conversation about books and movies and music which had carried them across the state line and into the outskirts of Knoxville.

The restaurant Chrys had chosen was quirky, and she hoped Dee would appreciate it. There were hipper, more expensive sushi places downtown, but the Asia Café had its own un-self-conscious charm. It wasn't hip; it was weird. Located on the south side of town, its clientele included Asian families ordering whole fish and hot pots, white working-class families eating sweet-and-sour whatever with fried rice and egg rolls, and burly bikers who availed themselves of the ninety-nine-cent Dragon Drafts at the bar. The décor was old-school Chinese restaurant kitsch, with lots of high-fiving cat figurines and red paper lanterns. The menu ran the gamut from Chinese and Chinese-American to Thai, Malaysian and Japanese. Everything was delicious.

Even though Meredith had admitted the food was good, she hated the Asia Café and preferred the dimly lit, sleek downtown places. (She had been particularly traumatized during a visit to Asia Café where a trio of drunken bikers had done a karaoke version of "Sweet Home Alabama.") Chrys wondered if part of the reason she was bringing Dee here was a personality test to make sure she was not like Meredith.

Once they walked in, the pretty hostess said, "Long time, no see."

"I know. I've been away for the summer at a place where there's no Asian food," Chrys said.

"Oh, we have to fix that, then," the hostess said, grabbing two menus and leading them to a red vinyl booth.

"Okay, I love this place already," Dee said. Her light blue off-the-shoulder top complemented her eyes. "It's so welcoming, and I was scoping out what people are eating, and it all looks great."

A young waiter with a scraggly beard and multiple piercings came by and said, "What can I get y'all to drink tonight?" While the restaurant's owners and chef were indeed Asian, most of the wait staff came from no farther east than east Tennessee.

"I'll have a Sapporo, please," Chrys said.

"Make that two," Dee said, then she grinned at Chrys and said, "Let's order a whole ocean's worth of sushi."

They just about did. The black lacquered plates spread out before them with delicate fish slices, neatly packed rolls, and dollops of electric green wasabi.

Chrys popped a tuna roll into her mouth, and its taste was bright and clean. "I don't think I could ever talk Nanny into trying sushi," she said. "I made tacos from a mix one night, and it was just about too adventurous for her."

"Is there any kind of sushi you won't eat?" Dee asked, picking up a chunk of yellowtail with her chopsticks. "I ask because I made the mistake of trying sea urchin roe once. Definitely an acquired taste which I have yet to acquire."

"I draw the line at octopus. Not because I find it gross but because octopi are too damn smart. Did you know that an octopus is capable of crawling up on land, finding a coconut shell, and taking it down into the ocean and making a house out of it? I refuse to eat any animal that may be smarter than I am."

Dee laughed. "I seriously doubt an octopus is smarter than you are."

"Maybe not. But it definitely would be smarter than some of my students."

A small stage was set up by the bar, and a squat fifty-something man in a sequined jumpsuit unceremoniously stepped up on it.

Dee leaned forward. "You see the Elvis guy, right? I mean, I'm not having a sushi-induced hallucination, am I?"

Chrys laughed. "No. He performs here pretty regularly. He calls himself Bobby the King. He's married to the hostess. He met her when he was in the service."

The squatty Elvis flipped on the karaoke machine and launched into a spirited version of "Burning Love," punctuated by karate kicks.

"You know, he's not bad," Dee said, reaching for a piece of dragon roll.

"No, he's pretty good, actually, even if he's seen a few more birthdays than the King ever did." Chrys felt that Dee had passed another unwritten test. When she and Meredith had eaten here for the third and final time and Bobby the King had taken the stage, Meredith had said she was "embarrassed for him."

The next number was "Can't Help Falling in Love With You." On the song's first line "Wise men say only fools rush in," Chrys had the same thought she always did when she heard the song: how strange it was that a song popularized by a folk hero like Elvis contained a quote from long-dead snob Alexander Pope. But as the song's words melted over her, she stopped thinking and started feeling.

More than she heard the music or tasted the hot wasabi and the cold beer, she felt Dee across from her—Dee with her honey-wheat hair down on her golden shoulders, Dee who was caring, Dee who was funny, Dee who was smart but didn't make a big deal of it. Chrys knew all the reasons it was dangerous to feel this way—she was still hurting from Meredith, she had no reason to think Dee had ever been anything but straight, she was in all likelihood setting herself up for more pain in the near or distant future—but she couldn't help it. Sitting across from Dee, with Bobby the King crooning in the background, she was like that little hen she had hypnotized, unable to look back or away, mesmerized by what was in front of her.

* * *

The atmosphere at Shakespeare on the Square was always a little chaotic. There were always quite a few people—college and high school kids and families out for some culture—who brought their folding chairs or blankets and settled in to watch the play. But since the square was full of restaurants and bars, there were also plenty of diners and drinkers wandering about, often talking over the play as they walked, and panhandlers who sometimes watched the play but mostly solicited donations from the audience. Since the original Shakespeare productions had also been in an outdoor venue, Chrys wondered if Elizabethan actors had had to compete with a similar level of chaos.

In terms of talent, the Shakespeare on the Square productions were kind of a mixed bag. The cast always included some talented regional actors like Aaron, but there were also high school kids, retirees, and a couple of rich dilettantes who helped bankroll the production. The Titania in this show, with her Botoxed complexion and perfectly highlighted hair, clearly fell into the dilettante camp, whereas the scenery-gnawing Oberon screamed retired high school drama coach. At first Chrys thought the talented teen actor playing Puck was a pretty boy but was delighted to learn it was actually a boyish girl.

Aaron was hilarious as Bottom, especially in the scene where he'd been turned into an ass, and Titania, enchanted by Puck to fall in love with the first creature she sees upon waking, swoons over his beauty. During the curtain call, he got one of the loudest rounds of applause.

Backstage, Chrys and Aaron ran into each other's arms. "I've missed you like crazy, honeybun!" he said.

"You too." Chrys's eyes were misty. "You did great up there."

"Thanks. I love doing comedy. Laughs are such instant gratification." He shifted his gaze. "Oh, you must be Dee. Come here and give me a hug. Handshakes are for trained dogs."

As Dee and Aaron hugged hello, Chrys noticed the actress who played Hippolyta holding hands with Puck. "Backstage romance?" she asked.

"Yeah, aren't they the cutest?" Aaron said.

"Too bad Hippolyta's not with a woman in the play, too," Chrys said. "I mean, she's the queen of the Amazons. Why the fuck does she want to marry a dude?"

The beautiful young man with a toasted-almond complexion who'd played Lysander joined them, and Aaron said, "Ooh, speaking of backstage romances, this is Jerell. Jerell, this is my friend Chrys and her friend Dee."

Jerell, who apparently didn't share Aaron's opinion that handshakes were for trained dogs, offered his hand to each of them and said, "I'm really disappointed I can't hang out with y'all tonight, but I've got another show to do."

"Are you in another play?" Dee asked.

Jerell smiled. "No, I do drag over at the XYZ. Y'all should come see me sometime."

"Definitely," Chrys said.

* * *

Back at his apartment, Aaron set a bottle of red wine and a plate of cheese and crackers on the coffee table. "Don't be shy about the wine. There's plenty more."

"You're such a bad influence on me," Chrys said.

"And you love it." Aaron filled their glasses. "Nobody has any responsibilities until tomorrow, right? We might as well indulge." He handed Dee a glass. "Are you okay? You're wearing this look like, 'Toto, I don't believe we're in Kentucky anymore.'"

Dee laughed. "I think I'm experiencing a very pleasant form of culture shock."

Chrys wondered what Dee meant—culture shock from moving from a rural setting to an urban one? Or culture shock from moving in such obviously gay circles? Instead of asking, she said to Aaron, "So Jerell is even more beautiful than you said he was."

"Well, words were inadequate. He's a beautiful person, too, not just on the outside. But when the outside matches the inside, you won't hear me complain." He sipped his wine.

"Are things getting serious?" Chrys asked.

"Well, you know how it is with us boys. We don't get too serious too soon. The first priority is to get the sex down pat, and once we do that, we try other things. Like talking." He reached out and touched Dee's hand. "I'm exaggerating, of course. Jerell and I do talk a lot. And I really like him. But he's going into his last year in the MFA program, and after that, he wants to try things in New York. So I don't know. I certainly wouldn't ask somebody to derail his career for a relationship with me." He nudged Chrys. "My name's not Meredith."

"Thank God," Chrys said.

"What do you mean?" Dee asked.

Chrys curled her feet under her on the couch. "When I met Meredith, I was an associate professor at Western Carolina State. I was right on track in my academic career. But I left rank and tenure and slid way down the academic food chain to be with her. And a few years later, she left me."

"Anna's dad left me," Dee said. "He'd left every other woman he'd ever been with, so I don't know why I thought I'd be any different." She drained her wineglass. "Sometimes I think there are two kinds of people: the leavers and the left. I know which kind I am."

"Me too," Chrys said. Meredith had been the worst leaver, but not the first.

"Me three," Aaron said. "Shit, I'd better find out which kind Jerell is."

"I wonder," Chrys said, the wine starting a pleasant buzz in her brain, "if two people who aren't leavers get together, if that means nobody ever leaves. They stay."

"That would be nice," Dee said.

"Things are getting entirely too philosophical in here," Aaron said. "I'd better get us another bottle of wine."

"I'm so glad you invited me this weekend," Dee said. "Between working and being a single parent, I don't get many chances to let my hair down."

Before Chrys could think of a response, Aaron swept in with a new bottle and said, "Well, we let it all hang out here. Curtains, carpet, you name it."

The second bottle of wine sent them into silliness, and after much giggling and guzzling, Aaron stretched—a bit theatrically, Chrys thought—and said, "Well, I think it's time for me to go night-night. I'll make you one of my famous breakfasts before you head out in the morning."

It was at least two hours before Aaron's usual Saturday night bedtime. Chrys knew he was making himself scarce so she and Dee could be alone. She didn't know if she loved him or hated him for it.

She and Dee were sitting in the same places on the couch, but without Aaron in the room, she felt like they were closer together. "I'm…I'm really happy you came with me," she said, her voice tight and shaky despite the three glasses of wine. "I was so nervous asking you…I was sure you'd say no."

Dee smiled, her lips stained purple from the wine. "I didn't even think about saying no. But I did wonder if it was a date or not."

Chrys felt her face heat up. "It's…it's whatever you want it to be."

"Well…I guess it doesn't matter what we call it. I just like being with you."

"I like being with you, too." What should she do? Take her hand? Lean in and kiss her? Chrys had never been the pursuer in a relationship before. Her relationships had always begun the same way…with her being the often oblivious pursuee.

"I guess it is getting pretty late," Dee said. "Maybe I'll go get changed for bed."

"Okay," Chrys said, wondering how she'd let the moment pass so quickly.

After Dee left, Chrys sat alone on the couch, the same couch where she'd sat alone for so many miserable hours after Meredith left her. It was easy to fall back into those feelings sitting here, feelings of being alone and unloved.

"Hey!" It was a stage whisper.

Chrys looked up, and there was Aaron in the doorway of his room, wearing a white T-shirt and lavender pajama pants, holding Miss Celie in his arms.

"What?" she said.

He put down the cat and sat next to her on the couch. "Get in there," he said, his head indicating the bedroom where Dee was.

"What?"

"Have you become hard of hearing? Get in there! She wants you to."

"No, she doesn't. She said it was late and she was changing for bed."

Aaron rolled his eyes. "Which is code for 'excuse me while I slip into something a little more comfortable.' For somebody with a PhD, you sure are dumb."

"I've never been the one who makes the first move."

"Which is a good thing since you sure do suck at it." He grinned. "Like when she said she didn't know if this was a date or not and you said 'It's whatever you want it to be.' What kind of Zen master bullshit was that?"

"You were eavesdropping on us."

He shrugged. "In an apartment this small, it's hard not to."

"Yeah, well, something tells me you weren't trying very hard not to."

Aaron stood. "I'm not going to allow you to sit on this couch and argue with me while there's a beautiful woman waiting for you behind that door. If there's a hair on your twat, you'll get in there."

Chrys couldn't help but laugh. "What the hell kind of expression is that?"

"One that's designed to move you from talk to action. Get in there, honeybun." He disappeared into his room and shut the door behind him.

Chrys took a deep breath. She wished she could knock back one more glass of wine for courage, but then again, it probably wasn't in her best interest to cross the line from pleasantly tipsy to sloppy drunk. She knocked on what, for a while, had been her bedroom door.

"Come in," Dee said. She was lying, half under the covers, in a cream-colored, spaghetti-strapped nightie. "Hey," she said.

"Hey. Is it okay if I sit down?"

Dee smiled, scooted over, and patted the spot next to her.

Chrys sat, turning a little to face Dee, whose honey-wheat hair fanned out across her pillow. "You're beautiful." The words came out before she could stop them.

Dee let out a nervous-sounding laugh. "What?"

In for a penny, in for a pound, Chrys thought. "You're beautiful, lying there in your gown, with your hair all spread out like that. You look like the queen of the Amazons. Or a goddess."

"Wow." Dee blushed and looked away, but her smile stayed. "I've never had a woman tell me I'm beautiful before. You are, too. Beautiful, I mean."

"Thank you." Chrys took another deep breath. "Listen... you know in the play tonight how the people in the forest were enchanted?"

Dee nodded.

"What if this was our night of enchantment? Then in the morning, if you want to say it was all a dream, you can."

"I wouldn't pretend it wasn't real."

"Well, what I mean is—if I were to lean over and kiss you— when we go back tomorrow to our regular lives, it wouldn't have to change anything if you didn't want it to." She looked into Dee's blue eyes, which were focused on her. "I...I mean, I don't know if you've ever been with a woman before."

"I haven't." She smiled shyly. "Well, not really. I mean, back in college there was this girl I guess I had a crush on, though I didn't realize it was a crush until we got drunk one night and ended up kissing, kind of a lot. It didn't go any farther than that, though."

So Dee had had a college near-lesbian experience, Chrys thought. It was something to build on anyway. "You know, the first time I answered the door and it was you standing there, I..." She fumbled for a verb phrase: wanted you? Loved you? "Uh..."

"I thought you were going to lean over and kiss me."

She might be inept at taking the lead, but by God, she knew how to take directions. She turned around, placed a hand on Dee's cheek, and pressed her lips to Dee's. Even though they were in bed, it was still a first kiss, soft and sweet.

The second kiss was longer, with Chrys's fingers tangled in Dee's hair, and Dee's strong arms wrapped around Chrys's shoulders. So many poets and singers, from Robert Frost to Johnny Cash, had described desire as fire, but it was only in this moment that Chrys understood this metaphor within her body. Heat radiated from Dee's touch, but heat also radiated from within Chrys, the consuming desire to touch and be touched.

"Was that okay?" Chrys asked, her breath short.

"Better than okay," Dee said, smiling.

"If I do anything that's not okay, just tell me," Chrys said. She had never been responsible for anyone's lesbian devirginization before, and she didn't want to pounce too aggressively and send Dee fleeing back to heterosexuality.

"I have a feeling," Dee said, reaching up to stroke Chrys's hair, "that everything from here on out is going to be better than okay."

"Well, I'll definitely strive for better than okay."

"Okay," Dee said, laughing.

Chrys and Dee's mouths pressed together, so did their bodies, their breasts, their bellies. Chrys became painfully aware that while Dee was wearing a whisper-thin nightgown, she herself was still fully clothed. "I have to get rid of some of these clothes," she whispered as they broke, gasping, from their kiss.

"Please do."

Chrys stood and unbuttoned her dress, feeling Dee's gaze upon her. She let the dress fall and climbed back into bed, glad that she had optimistically chosen to wear her pretty black bra and panties.

"Wow," Dee said and pulled her into bed.

Chrys lost her mind in the best possible way. She was a body discovering Dee's body, feeling the contours of her muscled thighs, the curve of her hips. When Dee slipped off her nightgown, her body was golden all over, her bronze-nippled breasts full but firm, the fuzz between her legs only a shade darker than the hair on her head.

"Honey," Chrys said, and it was an endearment but also a description. There was something about Dee that was like honey, the sweet, sun-kissed gold of her.

Chrys kissed her neck, her collarbones, her breasts and belly, every surface lovely and new. She didn't need to ask if what she was doing was okay because Dee's body told her all she needed to know. She kissed her way across Dee's belly to her hip, then her thigh, then settled in the soft nest between her legs. At the first stroke of her tongue, Dee gasped and clutched Chrys's hair. Chrys varied her pace from slow, sensual strokes to fast flicks, and then back to slow again until Dee's body quaked and she cried out loud enough to disturb the neighbors.

When Chrys moved up to lie beside her, Dee said, "So that's what all the fuss about oral sex is about."

Chrys laughed. "Surely you'd had it before."

"Yeah, but not like that. It was always some dude lapping away like a dog at a water dish. They were never even in the zip code of the place that would get me off. But what you did"—she touched Chrys's cheek—"was like music." She ran a finger under Chrys's bra strap. "So why are you not naked yet?"

"I guess I just hadn't gotten around to it." She sat up to unhook her bra. She was always a little self-conscious about the size of her breasts. "They're big," she said, as she let the bra fall away.

"They're perfect," Dee said.

Chrys lay back, and Dee kissed and stroked her. Dee hooked her thumbs in the waistband of Chrys's panties, then stopped. "You realize that once I get these off, I have no idea what I'm doing."

"Sure you do," Chrys said. "Just do what would feel good to you."

Chrys felt the slide of her panties down her hips, her thighs, her ankles. Dee breathed what sounded like a sigh of appreciation before she started stroking her, first lightly with her whole hand, and then with one finger pulsing on her most sensitive spot. Chrys wanted the feeling to go on forever, but then the ripples of pleasure turned into great crashing waves.

"Did I do okay, teacher?" Dee asked as she snuggled beside her.

"If there were a grade higher than an A plus, I'd give it to you."

They cuddled for a while in silence, and then Dee murmured, "Willadeen."

"What?"

"Willadeen. You know how I told you I only tell my full name to people I'm really close to? Well, I think we're definitely close enough now that I can tell you my given name is Willadeen. My dad's William, and my mom's Deena, thus my fate was sealed."

Chrys laughed but restrained herself from laughing too hard. "Well, it's a pleasure to meet you, Willadeen." She closed her eyes and imagined one of those airbrushed custom bumper plates redneck couples put on their pickup trucks. In airbrushed cursive against a sunset background, it read, "Chrystal + Willadeen."

CHAPTER FOURTEEN

The silence was driving her crazy.

The morning after her and Dee's *Midsummer Night's Dream* had been pleasant. Aaron made blueberry pancakes, and they laughed and chatted through breakfast. On the ride home, though, Dee grew quieter as they reached the state line. After they crossed the "Welcome to Kentucky" sign, Dee said, "You know, what happened last night was really huge for me. It's going to take me a while to process it."

"I understand," Chrys said, a knot forming in her stomach.

"I mean, I've gone through some big changes the past couple of years, and now this, too."

"You make it sound like some disaster's befallen you." Chrys saw a dead possum on the road and felt like roadkill herself.

"I don't mean it that way," Dee said, running her hand through her hair in obvious frustration. "I just mean this changes the way I think about myself and my life and what I want. I'm…I'm overwhelmed."

"You had a good time last night, though, right?" She didn't want to sound needy, but she couldn't help it.

"I had a great time last night. I think that's why I'm overwhelmed." She laughed a little, but it sounded like nervous laughter. "I just need to think things through for a few days."

"Okay. How about I leave you alone until Nanny's appointment on Thursday?"

"Okay."

And so for the past two days, there had been silence from Dee but the noise of a million "what ifs" in Chrys's head. "Good lord, honeybun," Aaron said when she vented her anxiety on the phone. "It took you years to come out. You're expecting her to do it in a twenty-four-hour period."

She knew he was right, knew she was being irrational to want Dee to pledge her everlasting love to her after just one night. And what an idiot she'd been to tell Dee that their night together didn't have to change anything between them. Of course it did.

Right now Chrys was sitting at the supper table with Nanny, picking at a plate of macaroni and cheese.

"You feeling poorly?" Nanny asked.

"What?"

"It just seems like for the past couple of days you ain't had much of an appetite and you've had this kind of faraway look about you. I just wondered if you might be coming down with something."

Chrys had been trying to act normal around Nanny but had obviously failed. Trying to act normal was probably always a failure, just like trying to have a good time. "I'm just a little out of sorts. Maybe I've got a summer cold coming on."

"Maybe so," Nanny said. "The way you've been acting... all dreamy and not eating...if there was anybody around here for you to have taken a shine to, I'd say you was in love."

It took a tremendous amount of effort for Chrys to fake a laugh.

* * *

Chrys ran hot, soapy water over the breakfast dishes and looked at the clock for the hundredth time this morning. 8:42. Nanny's appointment was in a little more than an hour. What if Dee was cold to her when she showed up? Or—and here was a possibility that was even worse—what if she opened the door to find a different physical therapist because Dee had fled entirely? Tears sprang to her eyes. She was hurting from a rejection she hadn't even experienced yet.

She washed the dishes and told Nanny she was going to take a quick shower. She let the hot water pound her shoulders, trying to force herself to relax. As she washed her body, she remembered the feeling of Dee's hands on her, sure she would never know that pleasure again.

It was hard to decide what to wear. She didn't want to look like a slob because that would make her more easily rejectable, but if she made an effort to look her best, she would seem desperate to please. She finally settled on a denim skirt, a plain white T-shirt, silver hoop earrings, and the holy trinity approach to makeup.

The next time she passed the clock it was 9:22. She settled in the living room with Nanny and pretended to watch some inane morning talk show with grinning hostesses who seemed to find everything—from low-cal versions of Mexican favorites to an appearance by some reality star Chrys had never heard of—equally thrilling. When the doorbell rang, she jumped as though it was connected to an electrode that shocked her.

Dee stood in the doorway in her green uniform shirt. She gave a shy smile. "Hi."

"Hi." Chrys's face was too tense to return the smile.

"So after I work with your nanny we can talk, okay?"

"Okay." In Chrys's experiences, talks that were announced before they actually occurred were never good.

As Nanny and Dee worked together, Chrys paced the floor of her room. She made herself sit down and try to read an article from an issue of *Vanity Fair* Aaron had given her, but she couldn't concentrate. Desperate for some physical activity to occupy her, she unmade her bed so she could remake it. When

Dee's voice finally called out, "We're done," she jumped as though the moment she'd been anticipating for the past hour came as a total surprise. She took a deep breath, slipped on her sandals, and walked into the living room, where Nanny was relaxing with a bottle of water.

"She did a great job today," Dee said in a pleasant but professional voice that gave nothing away.

"And she plain wore me out," Nanny said. "Chrystal, can you walk her to her car?"

Once they were out in the yard, they stood for an awkward moment, looking at each other and then looking away.

Chrys wanted to touch Dee, to stroke her hair, but she willed her arms to stay at her sides and said, "I've missed you these past few days."

Dee reached out and took Chrys's hand. "I've missed you, too."

Once Dee's hand was in hers, Chrys didn't let go. "Would you like to sit at this incredibly uncomfortable concrete picnic table and talk for a few minutes?"

Dee nodded. When she sat, she said, "Nothing says comfort like concrete." But then her face turned serious. "Listen, I appreciate that you've given me a few days to think about things. I know it was hard, being left in the dark like that."

"I'm sure it was no picnic for you either, trying to figure things out." She thought of where they were sitting and smiled. "I said no picnic, yet here we are at a picnic table."

Dee smiled back. "I guess being a mom, the first thing I think about is how this would affect Anna. She's been through a lot of emotional upheaval the past few years—being picked on at school, the divorce. And then since the divorce, her dad hasn't been as attentive to her as I wish he would be. And there was the move here. That's a lot of change."

"It is," Chrys said, trying to prepare herself for rejection.

"I don't want to rush her into any more big changes. And you're just coming off a bad breakup. You probably shouldn't be rushing things either."

"Wise men say only fools rush in," Chrys half-whispered.

"Yeah. So what I'm wondering is…do you think we could just kind of date a little? Take things really slow?"

Chrys felt like she'd been awaiting the sting of a whip, only to get a pat on the back instead. "Really? You want to…date me?" She sounded fifteen, but she didn't care.

Dee broke out in a full-fledged grin. "Yeah, I do. But let's go slowly, okay? This is all really new."

"Slugs move faster than I will, I promise." Chrys was smiling and tearing up at the same time.

"And I haven't talked to Anna about this yet. I thought maybe we could spend some more time with her together first…let her get to know you better. She already likes you."

"And I like her," Chrys said, meaning it.

"She's not been raised to be a homophobe, but there's a big difference between accepting your friends and accepting your mom."

"True. And when kids think about their parents' sexuality, there's always a certain ick factor, no matter what the parents' sexual orientation is."

"True," Dee said. "Wow. I feel good."

"Me too." She reached across the table and took Dee's hand. "Hey, what if you and Anna come to the family cookout tomorrow night? Nanny would love to have you there, and I guarantee you'll find meeting the rest of my family… interesting. Plus, since it's the Fourth, I'm pretty sure illegal fireworks will be involved."

Dee grinned. "Okay, but only if the illegal fireworks will be shot off by people who have consumed an unwise amount of alcohol."

Chrys pictured the Daddy-and-Dustin pyrotechnics of Independence Days past. "I can guarantee it."

If taking it slow was the rule, Chrys couldn't think of a better invitation than to one of her family's cookouts. Short of going deer hunting with her daddy, one would have to work hard to come up with an idea for a less romantic outing.

* * *

Until she arrived at the Fourth of July cookout, Chrys didn't realize that she was supposed to dress for the occasion. Her mom was wearing a T-shirt with a sequined American flag, and Peyton was sporting a stars and stripes bikini along with her tiara. "Look at me! I'm Miss America!"

"You sure are, honey," Nanny said.

"Miss America is the princess of America," Peyton said.

"We don't have princesses in America," Chrys said. "But we have women who are governors and senators, and one day we'll even have a woman president."

Peyton gave Chrys a look that was not dissimilar to that of the students who found her lectures to be an unwelcome distraction from their texting. "I got red, white, and blue ribbons to put around the dogs' necks if I can catch 'em." She ran off in the direction of the nearest Chihoundhound.

"I really wish she'd find some women to look up to who aren't beauty queens or princesses," Chrys said to Nanny.

"Oh, that's just her age," Nanny said. "When you was four you wanted to be a trapeze artist."

Chrys laughed. "That's a fine career for someone who's terrified of heights."

Nanny smiled. "You wasn't thinking about the heights. You was thinking about the costumes. We took you to see the Clyde Beatty Circus when it came to Morgan, and you thought the trapeze artist was the prettiest thing in the world on account of her sparkly outfit. Little girls love sparkles."

"And I guess women senators don't wear sparkles or tiaras."

"I reckon not," Nanny said. "But maybe Peyton'll grow up and change that."

"Hey, Sissy, catch!" Dustin said and tossed a PBR tallboy at her.

She cracked it open. "Sorry to sin right in front of you, Nanny."

"That's all right, honey. I let God be the judge."

"Thanks, I guess." If there was a God, surely He didn't keep track of such minutiae as one's PBR consumption. And if He did, Daddy was way ahead of her. He had an empty can at his feet and a full one in his hand as he manned the grill. There were deer burgers as usual, but since it was a holiday, there were hot dogs, too, and chicken legs.

Chrys followed her mom into the kitchen to help carry out the side dishes, a larger array than usual: potato salad, deviled eggs, baked beans, cole slaw and some kind of Jell-O and fruit cocktail suspension. "This is quite a spread," Chrys said.

Her mom smiled. "Well, it's the Fourth of July, so we might as well put on the dog. Besides, if your daddy and Dustin blow us all up with fireworks later, this'll be the last meal we ever eat."

Amber laughed. "I didn't know Dustin was such a pyro when I married him."

"I could've told you," Chrys said, picking up the tray of deviled eggs. "When he was little, his favorite thing to do was tie firecrackers to plastic toy soldiers and blow them up."

When Chrys carried the eggs to the table outside, she sucked in her breath a little at the sight of Dee, who was talking with Nanny. Dee's tan legs were lovely in shorts, and Chrys had to remind herself not to stare. Anna was sitting on the ground laughing, while three Chihoundhounds competed for space on her lap.

Peyton ran up to Chrys. "Who's that girl?"

"That's Anna. She's my friend Dee's daughter."

Peyton looked at Anna with something like awe. "She's really big."

"Yeah, she's eleven. She's also really nice. I bet she might help you get those ribbons on some of the doggies' necks."

Peyton ran over to Anna, who greeted her with a shy smile.

"Hey," Dee said, smiling at Chrys. "I brought a salad."

Chrys wanted badly to hug Dee, but she also didn't want them to be conspicuous. So she took the bowl from Dee's hand, letting her pinkie graze Dee's in the process. Somehow this felt very pleasantly naughty. "Wow, an actual green salad.

I don't think we've ever had one of these at a cookout before. Unless green Jell-O counts."

"I'm pretty sure it doesn't," Dee said.

After Daddy brought the meat from the grill, they filled their plates buffet-style and sat at the long wooden picnic table Daddy had made when Chrys was a kid.

Dee sat across from Chrys and between Anna and Chrys's mom. Chrys, Dee and Anna were the only ones who had taken any of the green salad.

"Good bread, good meat, good God, let's eat," Daddy said.

"That ain't no kind of prayer," Nanny said.

"The Lord knows I meant no harm," Daddy said. "He's got a sense of humor, or else why'd he make me?"

"Our guests must think we're awful the way you're cutting up," Chrys's mom said to Daddy. Then she turned to Dee. "I think it's just wonderful that you're a physical therapist. It must make you feel good helping people that way."

"It's a good job," Dee said.

"I always wanted to be a nurse," Chrys's mom said. "But then I got married and had kids and never got around to it."

This was the first Chrys had ever heard of this. "Really? You never told me that."

Mom grinned and shrugged. "Well, I didn't want you to get the wrong idea—to think I had regrets."

"How come you didn't go back to school once Dustin and I were school-aged ourselves?"

"Well," Mom said, "by that time I figured I should just go ahead and get a job…let you grow up and be the college-educated one."

"'Cause it sure wasn't gonna be me," Dustin said, and everybody laughed.

"I'm sure you would've been an excellent nurse," Dee said to Chrys's mom once the laughter had died down.

"Well, you know after the kids was grown, I didn't want her to get bored," Daddy said. "So I cut my arm off so she could nurse me. Now if that ain't love, I don't know what is."

After dinner, as the women were cleaning up, Anna came up to Chrys. "Mom told me there are chickens and a pig over at your nanny's place," she said, her face serious. "I wondered if you might take me over to see them."

Chrys was a little surprised but tried not to show it. "Sure. It's an easy walk. We just have to go across a field."

Anna nodded. "Okay."

They set off. "I loved the first Harry Potter book, by the way," Chrys said. "I lost an entire night's sleep finishing it."

"I'll send the next one in with Mom when she comes to do your nanny's therapy. They get better and better." She walked a few steps and turned around, surveying the field. "This reminds me of the moors in *Jane Eyre*," Anna said. "That's what I'm reading right now."

Chrys felt a little thrill of bookish-girl kinship. "I love *Jane Eyre*. It's one of my absolute favorites."

"Mine too," Anna said. "But I still can't figure out why Jane is so in love with Rochester. I think he's kind of a douche."

"Well, yeah, he is, isn't he?" Chrys said, laughing. "What was it with the Brontes anyway? Have you read *Wuthering Heights?*"

"Not yet."

"Well, Heathcliff and Cathy are both douches."

They walked for a couple of minutes in silence, and then Anna said, "I've seen chickens before."

"What?" Chrys said, confused.

Anna stopped walking. "I don't care if we see the chickens or not. I used seeing the chickens as a pretense to talk to you one-on-one."

Chrys's stomach buzzed, a beehive of nerves. "A pretense? I wish my college freshmen had a vocabulary as good as yours." Her attempt to diffuse the tension with humor and flattery had obviously failed. Anna didn't crack a smile.

"You and my mom...you're dating, right?"

In her shock, Chrys randomly remembered a line from a famous Monty Python skit: "No one expects the Spanish

Inquisition!" She cleared her throat. "Uh, well, sort of. How did you figure it out?"

"I'm not stupid."

"I'm sure no one has ever said you were."

Anna picked a piece of long grass and started fidgeting with it. "When Mom came back from that trip she took with you, she acted weird. She was nervous, she hardly ate anything. She'd get up in the middle of the night and sit at the computer for hours. And if I came to check on her, she always acted startled and minimized whatever she was looking at. I could tell from the search history, though, that she'd been Googling *lesbian*."

Chrys gave a nervous laugh. "Wow, you're quite the intrepid spy, aren't you?"

"I didn't mean to spy. The word just popped up when I was Googling something else. And then the other day after she'd seen you, she was all happy and not acting nervous anymore and she mentioned you, like, three times at dinner."

"So has this kind of freaked you out?" Chrys said. Anna's tone had been so even she couldn't tell where this was going.

"It surprised me, I guess, but I'm okay with it. Mom's taste in men has always been questionable. But based on you, her taste in women seems to be better."

Chrys let out the breath she'd been holding. "Thanks. So your mom doesn't know you know?"

"Nope." A tiny smile crossed her lips.

"Are you going to tell her?"

Her smile grew wider. "What, you don't think I should let her sweat it out a little longer?"

Chrys returned the smile. "And have the poor woman worry herself to death over how to tell you something you already know?"

"I'll tell her. Tonight when we get home and have our bedtime cup of tea."

Chrys couldn't help imagining herself there with them sharing in this cozy ritual. "Good." She'd so thoroughly lost track of time that she had no idea if the two of them had been gone long enough to have looked at the chickens and the pig. "So," she said, "you've seen chickens, but have you ever seen anybody hypnotize a chicken?"

Anna laughed. "Chickens can be hypnotized? Really?"

"Really. And you're talking to a highly seasoned chicken hypnotist. Would you like a demonstration?"

"Sure."

They walked across the field, side by side.

CHAPTER FIFTEEN

"Anna's sleeping over at her friend's house tonight," Dee had said over the phone this morning. "If your mom can look after Nanny, do you want to come over for dinner?"

It was strange how Chrys's comings and goings depended, as in adolescence, on checking in with her mom, but now it was because Chrys was a caregiver, not a receiver. Even so, she had still felt like an excited kid when her mom said yes.

Dee met her at the door wearing a soft purple sundress. Her hair was down, and her feet were bare. Chrys wanted to kiss her but remembered Dee's admonition that she wanted to take things slow. But before Chrys could decide what move to make, Dee's lips were against hers in a soft kiss.

"Hi," Dee said.

"Hi." Chrys smiled as Dee took her hand and led her into the house.

"We're having pasta with vodka sauce but without the vodka," Dee said, leading her toward the kitchen. "One of the hazards of cooking in a dry county."

"So it's the Baptist version of vodka sauce?" Chrys said.

"Yep." Dee turned on the heat under a pot of water. "The vodka doesn't make as much of a difference in the taste as you'd think, though. And I did dust off a bottle of wine I had lying around if you'd like a glass."

"Twist my arm."

"How about I twist this corkscrew instead?" As she worked on the bottle, she said, "Hey, I need to tell you something. Anna figured out the deal between you and me on her own. Apparently I was nowhere near as subtle as I thought I was being. Well, either that, or I need a dumber kid." She poured the wine and handed her a glass.

Chrys didn't know if she should say anything about her own conversation with Anna. "She's okay with it, though, right?"

Dee took a sip of wine. "She's totally okay—with it. With you. With us. Really, since the divorce I had only gone out on a handful of dates, and they were all disasters. She says she's glad I'm finally showing some taste."

Chrys laughed. "Well, that's kind of her." She sipped her wine and thought. She didn't want to rat out Anna, but she didn't want to keep secrets from Dee either. "She talked to me, too, last night at the cookout. I made her promise to talk to you right away, so you wouldn't waste any time worrying how to tell her."

Dee whooped with laughter. "That little drama queen! I guess I took her out of her natural habitat of other gossipy preteens, so now she has to get her drama fix from adults. You weren't offended, were you?"

"Not at all. It was kind of great, actually. The way she lured me off on a ruse for a secret conversation. No wonder she loves gothic novels. She has an appetite for intrigue." Chrys was already feeling Anna tugging at heartstrings she didn't know she had. "She's a cool kid. I hope she and I can get to be good friends."

"I think she'd like that. She's always been the kind of kid who finds adults more interesting than children. She's struck up this friendship with this girl up the road, but Holly's two years older than she is." Dee stirred the pasta. "Honestly, I think Anna was born a forty-year-old English professor."

The vodka sauce was delicious, even without the vodka. They sat across from each other in the kitchen with the lights turned down and a candle glowing on the table. "This is a little more romantic than the cookout at my parents'," Chrys said.

Dee smiled. "Oh, I don't know. Nothing says romance like a fresh-grilled deer burger."

"Meredith, my ex, only made it to one family cookout. She was a suburban girl, and the deer burgers just about did her in."

"Coward," Dee said, refilling their wineglasses. "Well, I plan to come back to as many family cookouts as you'll let me. They're good folks, your family."

"They are. We don't see eye to eye on everything, and their views on religion and politics are way different than mine. But they're still good folks."

"You said Nanny doesn't know you're gay. But the rest of your family?"

Chrys chewed thoughtfully. "They know. It took me forever to get up the nerve to tell them, but they were each accepting in their own way. Dustin doesn't think what any adult does with another adult is anyone's damn business. Mama cried a little because there'd be no wedding or babies, but she said I should live my life for my happiness and not hers. I thought her religion might cause some trouble, but she said God made me and God doesn't make mistakes."

"What about your dad?"

"He was the toughest sell, no doubt. He had to go fishing and think about it, but he finally got it to jibe with his other cockeyed ideas about religion and politics. You should've heard him during the George W. administration: 'Dick Cheney goes hunting and loves his gay daughter, and so do I.'"

Dee laughed.

"Overall, they were as cool about it as I could have reasonably expected them to be. I don't know why I wasted so many years being afraid of telling them." She mopped up the rest of the vodka sauce with a piece of French bread. "You know, it's like I spent so much of my life feeling so different from them and wanting different things than what they wanted. I wasn't going to be a country girl but a city girl. I wasn't going to be working class but professional. I wasn't going to be religious but I could be spiritual. And I still feel that way, but now that I'm older, I see that because these are the people I came from, they're a part of me, and I'm a part of them. Does that make any sense?"

Dee nodded. "It does. That's why I couldn't stand to see Papaw's farm get sold off for mineral rights."

"Exactly. I feel like I spent most of my life saying 'not this, but that.' Now, though, I'm at the 'both and' stage. I don't have to reject everything I grew up with. I mean, it's okay to like sushi and cornbread, right?"

"Well, maybe not in the same meal." Dee smiled. "But I know what you mean. In a lot of ways, my upbringing was both urban and rural."

"So you've always been a 'both and' kind of girl."

"I guess, but"—she reached across the table and took Chrys's hand—"there are still plenty of changes going on in my life, too."

"Pleasant changes, I hope." Chrys stroked Dee's hand with her thumb.

Dee smiled. "Very pleasant and very surprising." She looked down at Chrys's hand in hers. "Listen, I know you probably need to get back to Nanny before too long, but I've got dessert and a tiny bottle of Prosecco." She took a deep breath. "And I thought a good place to enjoy these might be in bed."

Chrys's face heated up. "What happened to taking things slowly?"

Dee shrugged. "Well, my mind was all for it, but my body had other ideas."

Chrys was already out of her chair. "Well, I love your mind, but I think we'd better defer to your body on this issue."

"Agreed."

Standing next to the table, they met for the kind of kiss Chrys had wanted to give Dee when she walked in the door: a long, lingering liplock, their arms pulling their bodies tighter and tighter together. When they drew back, they were both out of breath.

"Well…let me get the wine and dessert," Dee said. She opened a cabinet and pulled out two stemmed champagne flutes.

"Wow, you own champagne flutes. I'm impressed."

Dee rolled her eyes. "Wedding present. I got rid of the husband but kept the presents."

"Good plan."

"I thought so, too." Dee opened the fridge and handed Chrys a chilled plate covered with wax paper. "No peeking. The dessert is a surprise."

Chrys followed Dee upstairs. Was there anything sexier than following a woman upstairs with the knowledge that the destination was her bedroom?

Dee's bed was old-fashioned and iron-framed, piled with pillows and draped with colorful throws. It looked exotic and inviting, like something in a gypsy caravan. Dee set the glasses on the bedside table and took the tray from Chrys. She opened the Prosecco and filled each glass with the fizzy golden liquid. Then she pulled the wax paper off the plate.

"My God," Chrys said. On the plate were a dozen plump, red, chocolate-dipped strawberries. "Now those are sexy."

"And," Dee said, "they're very juicy and messy, so maybe we'd better take off your dress so it won't get stained."

"How thoughtful of you." Chrys's heart pounded as Dee worked at the tiny buttons that ran down the front of her dress. Soon she was wearing only her peach-colored bra and panties.

"I'd better take mine off, too," Dee said, slipping her dress over her head. Her underwear was the same red as the strawberries.

Dee held a strawberry to Chrys's lips. When Chrys bit into it, the juice ran down her chin and throat, and Dee leaned forward and licked it off, starting at the base of her throat and ending at her lips. The pleasure was intense—the sweet chocolate and berry pulp, the warm wet of her lover's tongue, the sensation of tasting and being tasted at the same time.

Dee took another strawberry from the plate and tucked it into Chrys's cleavage just above the V of her bra.

"Oh, my," Chrys breathed.

"I had a fantasy about doing this." Dee nuzzled Chrys's breasts and bit the berry. She took the last of the berry in her mouth and unhooked Chrys's bra. "I want to do to you what you did to me before," Dee said. "But I'm not sure I know how."

"You've certainly given me no reason to doubt your skills."

They kissed, Dee pushing her on her back until she was lying on a pile of pillows like a lounging harem girl. Dee's mouth was warm, her tongue slippery and sure, stroking rhythmically, slow, then fast, then slow again until Chrys felt ripple upon ripple of pure physical joy.

When Chrys finally caught her breath, she said, "Well, there's no doubt about you knowing what you're doing."

Dee laughed and snuggled close. "I'll tell you, I had no idea what I'd be doing when I moved to Kentucky, but I never would've guessed I'd be eating strawberries from between a beautiful woman's breasts."

A beautiful woman. She'd said it like it wasn't a compliment but a fact. "I didn't think I'd be finding something like this here either."

Dee propped up on her elbow, smiling. "'Something like this' meaning something like me?"

"Well, something like…" She couldn't let herself say "love." Not yet. "Something like what I'm feeling right now… especially so soon after a bad breakup. I mean, it wasn't my intention to feel this way, but I couldn't make myself stay away from you."

"That's good. I don't want you to stay away."

"You know," Chrys said, "we're in that situation again where one of us is naked and the other isn't."

Dee grinned. "Should we remedy that situation?"

"I think we should." Chrys reached around to unhook Dee's bra. "And after what you did to me, I think I should return the favor."

Dee lay back on the pillows. "Please do."

Chrys did.

They lay in bed, legs entwined, nibbling strawberries and sipping Prosecco. "I have to ask you…" Dee lazily traced circles on Chrys's belly. "This isn't just some kind of summer fling rebound thing for you, is it?"

Chrys looked into Dee's eyes. So blue. "No. Am I a brief, post-divorce lesbian experiment for you?"

"No."

"Good. Our worst fears are allayed, then."

"Yep." Dee rested her head on Chrys's shoulder. "But still, you're just here till what, August?"

It was a grim reminder. "The fall semester starts August twenty-fifth. I guess I have to go back since there's the small matter of earning a living wage. Of course, we'll have to find somebody reliable to stay with Nanny before then."

"I'm working on that. Though maybe I shouldn't if it'll make you stay."

Chrys kissed Dee's forehead. "If I stayed here, I'd have to join the ranks of the Appalachian unemployed. My brother can't even find a labor job here, so what chance do I have? The only college for miles is Southern Baptist, and I don't think they're going to be clamoring for a faculty member with a lesbian studies background."

"You could be world's most erudite Walmart greeter. I know I'm being silly. I can't make you stay."

"It's not just the job thing, though. I spent so much of my life feeling like I couldn't live here and be the person that I am. Now it's better, but still, coming back to stay, there'd be a lot of baggage, you know?"

"I kind of figured you didn't want to add another trailer to your parents' backyard."

"I don't, but I can't say I'm too excited to be returning to a classroom full of texting, eye-rolling freshmen either."

Dee poured the last of the Prosecco into the glass they were sharing. "Are all of them texting eye rollers?"

"Not all of them. A few of them are older—moms going back to college now that their kids are in school. Some are vets on the G.I. Bill. The older students are the ones who really want to learn."

"Then focus on them, and ignore the texting eye rollers the same way they ignore you."

"You're right. It's so easy to focus on the things in life that annoy us, though." She laced her fingers through Dee's. "I've been thinking, too, about something else that might get me stimulated in a way teaching comp doesn't."

Dee grinned. "You mean like what we just did?"

"Well, that, too, but I meant intellectually stimulated." She was almost afraid to say it. Even though she'd been thinking about it a lot the past couple of weeks, she was scared the admission might be some kind of jinx. "I think I might have an idea for a new book."

"Really? What about?"

The idea had been simmering in the back of her brain for a month now, but this was the first time she had said a word about it. "I've been thinking a lot about Appalachian language. I've been writing down things Nanny says like 'crazy as a bessbug' or 'ain't got bat sense'—all these expressions that are dying out as people talk more and more like what they hear on TV. I've not figured out the angle all the way yet, but I think it'll be a work of scholarship but also of preservation. I don't know…it's about as far away from writing about lesbians on the Left Bank as I can get, but I've never written about anything that reflects where I come from, and I think I'd like to try."

"That's exciting. I can't wait to read it."

Chrys laughed. "Well, you'll have to. It'll be a long project. But I figure I can teach my classes and work on the book, and you and I can see each other on the weekends."

"Every weekend?"

"Every weekend."

Dee rested her head on Chrys's shoulder. "And what if, sometime down the road, we decide that weekends aren't enough?"

"We'll see from there."

Chrys couldn't believe she was in bed with another woman, talking about the future, but somehow it was right where she wanted to be.

CHAPTER SIXTEEN

Nanny was waiting in the glider on the porch. "Did you get enough to make us a cobbler?"

"I think so." Chrys held up the half-full bucket of blackberries. At Nanny's request, she had walked into the edge of the woods past Porkchop's pen where Nanny had correctly guessed the berries were getting ripe and juicy. "And my arms are scratched up enough that nobody can accuse me of buying the berries at the store."

"Didn't get bee stung, did you?"

"No."

"You'll want to check for chiggers, too."

Chrys laughed. "You know, I always used to complain about having to buy blackberries since I grew up picking them for free. But I guess picking them comes with a price, too."

"It does," Nanny said, her eyes crinkling as she smiled. "Especially if them chiggers gets up in your privates."

Chrys shuddered, then opted to change the subject. "So are you going to teach me how to make your famous cobbler?"

"Well, there ain't much to teach," Nanny said. "Just stir the berries up with half a cup of sugar and put 'em in a pan with some biscuit dough on top. You can sprinkle sugar on the biscuit dough if you want it to look fancy."

"You're making an assumption," Chrys said.

"How's that?"

"You're assuming I know how to make biscuit dough."

Nanny's mouth dropped open in shock. "You mean you're forty year old and don't know how to make biscuits?"

"That's about the size of it," Chrys said.

"Well, lawsy mercy, no wonder you ain't never got married. We've got to get you into the kitchen." Nanny reached for her walker and pulled herself out of the glider with a grunt. "I thought you helped me make biscuits when you was a little girl."

"I did, but just the rolling and cutting part."

Nanny shook her head as if this disservice from Chrys's childhood explained everything. "And your mommy never taught you?"

"She was always working. When she fixed biscuits, they were usually the canned kind."

"All right." Nanny sank into a kitchen chair. "You're gonna need to get out the flour, the buttermilk, the baking powder and the lard."

This last ingredient was disturbing. "Lard? Won't that stuff kill you?"

"Well, I'm eighty-nine years old, and I've been eating it all my life. You know how everybody always goes on about how tender and flaky my biscuits is?"

Chrys nodded.

"That's the lard."

"Lard it is, then."

Nanny gave orders from her chair as Chrys sifted and mixed. Her hands were goopy from dough, and her clothes were so whitened from flour she looked ghostly.

The phone rang. Chrys figured that by the time she got the goo off her hands, it would be too late to answer so she ran to the phone with doughy paws, leaving a trail of flour.

"May I speak to Mrs. Dottie Simcox?"

"Just a minute, please." Chrys carried the now-doughy cordless phone into the kitchen, mouthing "sorry" to Nanny as she handed it to her.

After Nanny said hello, she was silent for a minute. Then she said, "Well, that was about what we thought would happen, ain't it?"

This conversation was making Chrys nervous. The grammatically correct, non-Kentuckian voice on the other end of the phone definitely didn't belong to any of Nanny's friends. This call wasn't personal. It was official.

"Yes, I'm sure," Nanny said. "At my age, I don't want to put myself through anything like that." After a pause, she said, "I'll pray on it, but I don't think I'll change my mind. Thank you." She hung up and handed the phone back to Chrys.

"Nanny?" Chrys sank down in the chair across from Nanny. All of a sudden her knees had gotten weak.

"That was the doctor's office. You remember when you took me to have them tests done? They was calling about the little old tumor I got, but it ain't as little as it used to be."

"You mean cancer?"

Nanny nodded. "I've known about it for more than a year. I just ain't told nobody."

"Why not?" Chrys reached across the table to take Nanny's hand in her dough-sticky one.

"Well, you know how people get when they know you're sick. They act like if they say the wrong thing, you'll break like china. And you know what your mommy and brother would be like. They'd be on me to have the surgery, take the treatments…like my body could stand that at this age. But they'd want me to do it all, hoping for a miracle."

Chrys blinked away tears. "So why are you telling me?"

"Well, it'd be kind of hard for me not to after you heard half the phone call." Nanny's expression was calm, accepting.

She squeezed Chrys's hand. "But I figured you could handle it because you've always had good sense. The rest of the family uses their hearts before their heads."

"I'm not so sure I'm doing such a good job of that right now," Chrys said, reaching for a paper napkin to wipe her nose and eyes. She knew intellectually that Nanny couldn't live forever, but a world without Nanny seemed like a much sadder place to be. "Where's the tumor?"

"It's in my woman parts," Nanny said. "If I was childbearing age it would've grown a lot quicker, but that train left the station a long time ago." Nanny patted Chrys's knee. "Now don't be hanging no crepe yet, child. The doctor said I still might have another good year or two. And after that, I'll be in heaven with Chester and Ma and Pa and my sister, and that'll be even better."

"Yes," said Chrys, wishing she believed this were true. If there was a heaven, Nanny certainly deserved to go there and be joyfully reunited with everyone she had ever loved and lost.

"Now we'd better finish fixing that cobbler," Nanny said. "I want me a big bowl of it for dinner. We got any ice cream?"

* * *

Chrys almost felt too sad to eat, but if Nanny could stare mortality in the face and still eat a bowl of cobbler, then she would, too. It was delicious.

Chrys did the dishes while Nanny lay down for her nap. As she washed the purple juice from the berry bowl, she started to cry. She cried because of Nanny's cancer, because the day was drawing near when Nanny wouldn't be here anymore. And she cried because Nanny had trusted her enough to tell her her secret when she wouldn't tell anybody else.

When Nanny woke from her nap, Chrys asked if she wanted to have a glass of iced tea on the porch. They sat a while and watched the chickens peck.

"Are you feeling okay about spilling the beans to me today?" Chrys asked finally. "I promise I won't tell anyone."

"I know you won't. That's why I told you. The funny thing is, ever since I told you, I've felt so good—better than I've felt in a long time. It eats at you, having something inside that you ain't told nobody yet."

"It does." It seemed so unfair—Nanny had trusted her enough to share her secret, and yet one of the main facts of Chrys's life was still a secret from Nanny. "Nanny, I think I'd better tell you something about myself, too."

"You ain't sick, are you?" Her voice was sharp with worry.

"No, I'm not sick." She took a deep breath. Once she hadn't even been able to imagine having this conversation. Now she couldn't imagine not having it. "So the reason I've never gotten married isn't because I don't know how to make biscuits."

Nanny smiled. "I was just playing with you about that."

"I know. But the truth is that I've been evasive with you all these years saying I just haven't found the right man. For me, there isn't a right man. I'm a lesbian. I like women. I always have."

Nanny's eyes narrowed and she brought her hands together like she might be praying. "You mean you're like that Ellen on the TV?"

"Yes, like Ellen." Chrys mentally thanked Ellen for providing a likable lesbian public image.

"But you've got long hair and you wear dresses."

"Yes, but lots of lesbians do. Not all of us are…" She almost said butch but instead went for "boyish."

"Huh," Nanny said. She stared off into the distance for what was probably only a few seconds but felt longer. "My sister was like that. Not Irma, but my oldest sister, Hazel."

Today had certainly been a day for surprises. "Aunt Hazel was gay?" Chrys had never met her great-aunt Hazel, but she remembered her family getting a Christmas card from her each year. She knew her only as "Nanny's sister that lives in Michigan."

"She was. She was married to a man for a while. That was how come she moved to Detroit. He got a job up there after the mines closed. But she was unhappy, I reckon on account of being like she was. She ended up leaving him after about a year up there. After that she took up with a woman she met working in a restaurant. They stayed together till Hazel died, forty-some-odd years later."

"Really? Did everybody in the family know?"

"Ma and Pa knew and me and my brothers and sisters. Hazel never come right out and said what she was, but the longer she lived with that woman, the clearer it became. Finally Pa told her if she didn't change her ways the family wasn't gonna have nothing to do with her. He told her he'd never stop praying for her, though."

Chrys wondered how many women and men and girls and boys throughout time had heard similar things from their families. "So did you stop having anything to do with her after that?"

"Not all the way. I always sent her a card at Christmas and on her birthday and she did the same for me. But that was all. After she died, I knew two cards a year wasn't enough. We was so close when we was girls—as thick as thieves." For a few seconds, she had a faraway look in her eyes, but then she blinked hard, like she was coming back into the present. "They had her funeral in Detroit since nobody back home wanted nothing to do with her. I took the bus up there myself to go to it. I was the only real family she had there. Everybody else was her friends—women like her, I reckon. I went up to the woman she'd lived with and shook her hand and told her who I was." She looked off into the distance for a moment. "I know Pa thought he was doing the right thing, cutting her off like that. He said if you've got a tree with a rotten branch, you cut off that branch so it don't infect the whole tree. That's what he done to Hazel. But that's the way it was back then."

Chrys looked at Nanny. Her eyes were dry, but her mouth was set as if to keep her lower lip from trembling. "And what about now?"

"Well, I don't reckon you have to worry about nobody kicking you out of the family. I don't know, the Bible says it's a sin, but it says lots of other things is sins, too—some things people do all the time without even thinking about it. Since that day you went to church with me, I've been studying a lot on what you said—about how can just a few people in one little church go to heaven and everybody else end up in hell. I was praying on it, and it come to me that it's not man's job to judge other people. I can't judge you for being the way you are, child. Only God knows what's in your heart."

Chrys knew that this answer had been the result of a tremendous amount of thought on Nanny's part, and while she knew Nanny wouldn't be starting a branch of PFLAG anytime soon, it was still more acceptance than she'd let herself hope for. "Thank you, Nanny." She sniffed and dabbed at her eyes.

"Ain't no need for you to take on thisaway. You've always been a sensible girl. Now does your mommy know what you just told me?"

Chrys nodded. "Your daddy and your brother, too?"

"Yes."

"Huh," Nanny said. "How come I was the last to know?"

"Well…I was worried about how you'd react. I know how important your faith is to you, and for Free Will Baptists, being gay is about the worst kind of 'backslid' there is. Plus…" And here she started crying in earnest despite her nanny's admonition not to "take on." "I love you so much. You've always been my favorite, and I couldn't stand the thought of telling you something that might make you not love me anymore."

"Now you've always been a smart girl, but that's just plain foolish. You ought to know I'm always gonna love you no matter what." She opened her arms. "Come here."

Chrys bent over Nanny's rocker to hug her, but it wasn't close enough, so she got down on her knees. She sat with her head in Nanny's lap with Nanny's arms around her, and for those few minutes the years melted away and Nanny was in her early sixties, strong and mobile and cancer-free, and Chrys was a little girl.

CHAPTER SEVENTEEN

"I want to talk to both of you about something for a minute," Dee said.

Nanny had just finished her session and was sitting in her recliner. Chrys was sitting on the couch next to Dee but making an effort not to sit too close. The more intimate she and Dee became, the stranger it felt when Dee was acting in her "official capacity" as Nanny's physical therapist.

"A colleague of mine recommended a care agency that might be a good choice for when you have to go back to work, Chrys."

Nanny looked at Chrys. "Well, I hate to think about you leaving, but I know you've got to get back to your life. You didn't get all that education just to help old ladies use the toilet."

"It's been an honor helping you use the toilet, Nanny," Chrys said.

"This agency operates out of Morgan. My friend says several of her patients use them, and all their reports have been positive."

"They don't hire dopers that'll come in and steal my pills?" Nanny asked.

"They do a drug screening and a full background check on all their employees," Dee said. "And they only hire certified nursing assistants and LPNs." Dee passed a business card to Chrys. Their fingers brushed. "I already talked to the director, and she said there's availability starting in mid-August."

"We'll give them a call," Chrys said.

When she walked Dee to her car, Chrys said, "You know, there'll probably be a time before too long when Nanny will need a higher level of care."

"She told you, then?"

"You knew?"

Dee nodded. "Well, I have access to her medical records. I'm required to keep things confidential anyway, but she was still really insistent that I not tell anybody." Dee reached out and took her hand. "How are you doing with the news?"

"I'm okay. I mean, she's eighty-nine. I'd love to have her around forever, but I have to be realistic."

Dee smiled. "That's her exact attitude, too. It's funny, the two of you are different in the details, but when it comes to the important stuff, you're a lot alike."

"Well, some of the important stuff. You won't see me becoming a Baptist any time soon, and I don't think Nanny's going to start kissing girls. Speaking of which…" Chrys leaned over and brushed her lips against Dee's. "I've been wanting to do that all morning."

Dee's smile was shy. "And what if your nanny saw that?"

"Well, she'd be shocked I was kissing you, but she wouldn't be shocked I was kissing a girl."

"You told her? How did she take it?"

"She was surprisingly cool. She said she loves me no matter what."

Dee touched Chrys's cheek. "Actually, that's not so surprising at all."

* * *

Chrys had just finished her nightly phone conversation with Dee and was propped up in bed scribbling in the notebook she had bought for the purposes of planning her new project. Calling it a project was both more accurate and less intimidating than calling it her new book. It was in the earliest stages of development, and calling it a book would be like calling an embryo a child and putting it on the bus for elementary school.

She was slightly startled by the scratching on her window, but she had learned by now to expect to see her brother's face there, not a serial killer's. "You want a beer?" he mouthed exaggeratedly, pointing to two PBRs hanging from plastic rings.

She opened the window. "I'm in my pajamas."

"Come on out anyway. That's the great thing about being in the country. Ain't nobody out here to see you. You could come out here buck naked if you wanted to."

"I don't think I'll take you up on that," Chrys said, climbing out of the window.

"That wasn't an invitation, just a statement of fact." Dustin handed her a chilled can.

They walked over to sit at the picnic table, the grass cool under Chrys's bare feet. The black sky was sprinkled with stars. "I can never get over the night sky here. In the city you can't see the stars as well."

"That's too bad," Dustin said, looking up. "Peyton always says the stars look like rhinestones in a tiara, but it's always got to come around to princess stuff for her. I wonder if she'll miss them."

Chrys knocked back her first slug of PBR. It was a brand she would've never touched in Knoxville, but she was beginning to develop a taste for it. "Miss what?"

"The stars," Dustin said. "You said you can't see them so good in the city."

Chrys's hand froze in its route to convey the beer can to her mouth. "Dustin, are you—"

"I told Amber she could go ahead and take that transfer to Nashville. You're the first person I told we're moving."

"Really? What made you change your mind?"

Dustin grinned. "Well, being the bossy older sister you are, I know you'd like to think it was you that changed it. But it wasn't. It was Mommy."

This was strange news. Like most Appalachian mothers, Chrys's mom was a hen who liked to keep her chicks close to the roost. "But I thought Mom would throw a fit if you even talked about moving."

"She probably will. Like I said, she don't know yet."

"Then how—"

"It was at the cookout last week. You remember how Mommy was talking about how she always wanted to be a nurse but never got to on account of getting married and having to raise us. You remember that?"

"I do. That was the first time I ever heard her say anything about it."

"Me too." Dustin took a swig of his beer. "It got me to thinking…twenty, thirty years from now, I don't want Amber to be talking about how she wanted to be this or that but she never did 'cause she married me and got pregnant." He grinned. "Well, not necessarily in that order."

"Wow, Dustin. That's really thoughtful." Her brother had been the likable but impulsive manchild for so long, it was startling to hear such a mature statement from him.

"Didn't know I had it in me, did you?" He fished a Marlboro out of his back pocket and lit it. "I was thinking about Peyton, too. I want her to know she deserves a shot at being whatever she wants to be."

Chrys smiled. "Even if that's a princess?"

"I reckon. Don't know how much of a shot she's got at that one, though." He squinted through his cigarette smoke, a James Dean move he'd started practicing as a teenager. "To be honest, Sissy, I don't know how much of a shot Amber has at making it in music either. But I know it's the right thing to let her try. I've been going over to my buddy's a lot to use his computer and look up jobs in Nashville. I've applied for a few of them. This quickie oil change place wants me to come in for an interview next week when me and Amber go up there to look for a place to live."

"You've been changing the oil in cars since before you could legally drive," Chrys said. "You should be a shoo-in."

"I hope so. And I hope we can find an apartment we can afford that ain't too much of a rat trap. It'll be weird living in a little box stacked up against all these other little boxes full of people. It don't seem natural."

"It's not as bad as you make it sound," Chrys said. "And if things go well, maybe you can move to a house in a year or two. And if things go really well, maybe you can live in one of those big tacky country-music mansions."

"I don't know about that," Dustin said, grinning. "Me and Amber's talked a lot about it, and she wants to give this a try for a couple of years. If nothing happens, then she wants to go back to school. Maybe be a paralegal."

Chrys could easily picture Amber sitting in one of her English comp classes. "That's a good idea."

"Well, I figure either way it keeps her from working at the dollar store for the rest of her life. And me, I ain't exactly setting the world on fire staying here."

Chrys couldn't imagine how hard it was for Dustin to be setting off on such a new path after thirty-eight years of sticking with the familiar. "I'm proud of you, buddy."

"I don't know if you should be proud of me or not. I'm trying to do the best I can, but I'm scared shitless."

"That's how it feels to be a grownup."

"Is it?" Dustin laughed. "Well, hell, no wonder I've been putting it off for so long!"

* * *

Chrys snuggled under the covers, drowsy from the beer. She felt good. Sure, it was more likely that Amber would end up typing briefs in a law office than starring in videos on CMT. But it was right for her to try.

It was like love. It was possible that Chrys's relationship with Dee would end in heartbreak just like things had with Meredith. But if she didn't try, there was no hope at all, and what would be the point of that? Life was full of possibilities: heartbreaks and disappointments and setbacks and injustices. But there were wonderful possibilities, too, and the only chance you had to make them realities was to try, to hope, to love.

She slept soundly.

When the alarm on her phone told her it was time to wake, the screen was flashing "new message." She dialed her voice mail: "Honeybun, you've got to call me as soon as you get this. Call. Me."

Given the hours Aaron kept, it was highly unlikely he would be up at seven in the morning, but the obvious panic in his voice made Chrys dial his number anyway.

"Honeybun, where were you last night? I called and called."

"You must've called when I was outside with my brother. Are you okay?"

"I'm okay, but you're not gonna be when I tell you this. Are you sitting down?"

Chrys's stomach tightened. "I'm still lying down, actually."

"That's even better. So guess who came to see me for a massage?"

"I have no idea."

"Meredith."

"That's weird. She has a regular massage therapist she sees at her club."

"Honeybun, she didn't want me to wring her muscles. She wanted to wring me for information. About you."

Her anxiety was matched only by her confusion. Why would the dumper suddenly be interested in the dumpee? "Oh-kay."

"She asked if she could have your phone number, and I said I was pretty sure she was the reason you changed it. All this is while she's naked on the table, by the way, with me working on her, so you can imagine the awkwardness."

"Thanks for the visual."

"She asks if you're living with me, and I say no and that you're away for the whole summer. She's quiet for a while after that and I'm finishing up the massage and she finally says, 'Kentucky. That's where she is, isn't it?' I neither confirm nor deny it, which, of course, is pretty much confirming it. So I screwed up. I'm sorry."

"That's okay. You were blindsided."

"And now I'm trying to keep the same thing from happening to you."

"Did she give any indication what she might have wanted to talk to me about?" Chrys thought of the expensive gifts Meredith had given her over the years: the Tiffany jewelry, the high-end laptop, the surprise vacations to Europe and the Caribbean. Did Meredith want the stuff back? She couldn't return the vacations, of course, but anything else Meredith could have back. It was just like Meredith, to place conditions and an expiration date on her gifts...and her love.

"She didn't give me a fucking clue," Aaron said. "All I can tell you is that the way she said Kentucky and strode out of the salon, I wouldn't be surprised if you had a visitor sometime soon."

CHAPTER EIGHTEEN

Chrys fed the chickens. She dumped out a bucket of potato peelings and past-its-prime buttermilk for Porkchop. She went back in the house and refilled Nanny's coffee cup and started on the breakfast dishes.

She hadn't eaten any breakfast herself. Her stomach was too full of anxiety. Was Meredith going to show up on her doorstep, and if so, when? If she knew Meredith's take-charge-of-the-situation-right-now mentality, then it would be sooner rather than later. But what situation was Meredith trying to take charge of anyway?

She could head things off by calling Meredith herself, but no, that would just be making things easier for her. If Meredith wanted to see her, let Meredith put in the effort, even if the will-she-or-won't-she waiting game was going to put her in what Nanny called the nervous hospital.

After lunch (which she didn't eat any of either), Chrys jumped when the doorbell rang. It turned out to be the UPS man delivering a housecoat and some pig salt-and-pepper shakers that Nanny had ordered from the Harriet Carter catalog.

"Listen, they oink when you shake them," Nanny said, admiring her new purchase. "Ain't that cute?"

"It is," Chrys said distractedly.

"Child, is something the matter with you today? You're as nervous as a long-tailed cat in a room full of rockers."

Chrys had always liked that expression and let herself smile at it a little. "I am jumpy, aren't I? I don't know what's gotten into me." It was partially true. She didn't know why she was such a wreck. Even if Meredith was coming, it wasn't like she was coming to kill her.

"Maybe you're coming into the change of life. That makes some women take on funny."

"Well, I've definitely been going through some changes, but I don't think I've started that change yet."

After Nanny had settled in to watch *Wheel of Fortune*, the phone rang. Chrys picked it up and carried it away from the sounds of the overzealous crowd cheering the show's title.

"Chrystal, that ex"—Chrys's mother paused—"friend of yours just came to the door asking about you. Your daddy says if you don't want her coming around he's got ways of making sure she don't do it no more."

So here it was. "Tell Daddy not to shoot her. Where is she right now?"

"Standing on the porch."

Chrys sighed. "Tell her to come on over here. She drove all this way. I might as well find out what she wants. Thanks, Mom." She hung up the phone and said, "Nanny, I'm going to have company for a few minutes. Someone from Knoxville. We'll talk out on the porch."

"You'uns can talk in here if you want. I can go to my room."

Chrys had no desire for Meredith to invade the peacefulness of Nanny's little house. "Thanks but no. Whatever this is going to be it'll definitely be an on-the-porch kind of conversation."

Nanny looked at her hard. "Child, is this something I ought to be worried about?"

"Not all. You don't need to worry about anything except how stupid these contestants on *Wheel of Fortune* are."

There was a knock at the door. Chrys took a deep breath and went to answer it.

It was easy to forget how good-looking Meredith was. There was a butchness to her looks, but it took on the air of a beautiful boy rather than a handsome man. Her jawline was defined but still soft, and she wore her hair bobbed like an effete young gentleman's in an Evelyn Waugh novel. Today she was wearing a button-down shirt and khakis that were impeccably ironed and, Chrys knew, of high-quality but not flashy brands.

"Hi," Meredith said, sounding a little more uncertain than Chrys was used to.

"Hi," Chrys parroted back. "I thought we could talk on the porch. Could I get you some iced tea or water?"

"Do you have a beer?"

"Not in Nanny's house."

Meredith nodded. "Okay. Water then, thanks."

"Have a seat on the porch. I'll be right out." She figured Meredith had to notice she'd been relegated to the porch two times in a row as if she were a vampire no one wanted to invite inside. When Chrys filled the water glass, her hands shook.

She took the glass outside, handed it to Meredith, and sat down in the rocking chair beside her. It was laughable, the two of them on the porch in their rockers like Ma and Pa Kettle. "So," Chrys said, "I haven't pawned any of the jewelry you gave me so you can have it back if you want it. I'd like to keep the laptop, but I'm willing to pay you for it."

Meredith looked at her, an eyebrow raised. "Is that what you think this is about? Getting back the gifts I gave you?"

"I have no idea what this is about. I was just guessing."

Meredith shook her head. "Well, you guessed wrong. Do you really think I'm the sort of person who would ask you to return gifts I gave you out of love?"

At the sound of the word "love," a lump formed in Chrys's throat. "I'm not sure what kind of person you are, Meredith. I thought I knew, but I was wrong."

Meredith set her water glass on the porch railing. "Okay, how about this? I'm the kind of person who makes mistakes. And in the case of you and me, I'm the kind of person who fucked up spectacularly."

"So…you're apologizing." She had noticed the uncharacteristic unsteadiness of Meredith's hand when she had set down the glass. This was the first time she'd ever seen Meredith act nervous.

"I don't know. I mean, I am, but an apology is inadequate. I want you to know I made the biggest mistake of my life when I left you, and the reason I left you…well, that's all over."

"You broke up?" Talk about a short-lived relationship. They hadn't even lasted the summer.

"Well, the most accurate way of expressing it is to say she broke up with me." Meredith smiled sheepishly. "Go ahead and laugh. I know I'd want to if I were you."

Chrys didn't laugh, but the corners of her mouth did twitch a little. "What happened?"

"What happened was that there was no substance to our relationship. I was enamored with her youth and beauty, and she was enamored with my position and power. We weren't in love with each other. We were in love with the qualities we saw in each other that we wanted for ourselves."

"But you are beautiful." Chrys hadn't really meant to say it, but there it was.

Meredith looked at her, her gaze soft. "Thank you for that. But I'm not young anymore, am I? I'm ashamed to admit it, Chrys, but you were the victim of my midlife crisis. If I were a guy, I probably would've gotten hair plugs and a convertible in addition to the younger woman. I never thought myself to be prone to cliché behavior, but when I crossed paths with Audrey, it felt fresh and exciting…not like a script that millions of people had acted out millions of times before." She shook her head. "I should never judge my patients again who are so desperate to lift and tuck away the ravages of time. I was doing the same kind of thing by following youthful pheromones."

"Well, we're all animals." Chrys watched the hens congregate around the rooster in the yard. "We justify what our hormones tell us in the name of love."

"You don't believe in love anymore?"

"I didn't say that. I just meant humans have a tendency to mistake desire for love."

Meredith nodded gravely. "It's a mistake I'm truly sorry I made. Can you forgive me?" Her eyes were dry, but her jaw was set the way that meant she was struggling with her emotions. In their five years together, Chrys had only seen Meredith cry twice.

Chrys had had so many angry fantasies about what she would say if she and Meredith ever came face to face again, but there was nothing she could say about Meredith that was harsher than what Meredith had just said about herself. Meredith had taken all her best lines. "What you did to me hurt like hell. It still hurts. But I forgive you."

"Thank you." Tears shone in Meredith's eyes but did not fall. "And listen, I know I wasn't appreciative enough of the sacrifices you made by giving up your university job and moving to Knoxville. I know you derailed your career by coming to be with me, and I know teaching five sections of freshman comp at a fifth-rate college is a major grind. I don't think I was always as sympathetic as I could've been."

"You don't have to feel sorry for me. I made my choice. And you know what? I probably spent too much time feeling sorry for myself. I mean, unlike my mom, I got all the education I wanted. Unlike my brother, I have a job. And unlike Nanny, I have my health. But not one of them spends a second on self-pity. Me? I wasn't suffering. I was just inconvenienced. I've been a whiny bitch."

"Not at all," Meredith said, though her little laugh made Chrys wonder if she thought otherwise. Meredith stood up and leaned against the porch railing, knocking the water glass off the porch with her hip. "Oops. That wasn't the effect I was going for."

"It's okay. No need to cry over spilled…water, right?"

"Right. Listen. There was something I wanted to talk to you about. A job, actually."

This was certainly the last thing she'd been imagining. "A job?"

"I've been doing some post-mastectomy reconstruction for a patient who's the director of undergraduate studies in the English department at UT. She's a dyke, and we've gotten kind of chummy. Don't raise your eyebrows—not that kind of chummy. Anyway, she let me know that a member of their department just took a job at another university without any notice and left them in the lurch. They're desperately scrambling to find a replacement. I told her I knew someone who would be perfect."

"You did?" As the state flagship school, the University of Tennessee would be a great move up, not only from Hill College, but from Western Carolina State, too.

"I did, and she's very interested. Since this is a desperate, last-minute situation, they're hiring it as a one-year interim position, but there'd be the option of renewal if you were good. And I know you are."

It was almost too much for Chrys to take in. "What…what would I be teaching?"

"Well, first of all, you'd teach four classes instead of five. There'd be one section of comp but also a couple of British Lit surveys and one class for majors on the international novel."

"Wow." For an English professor, she was terribly inarticulate. "Wow."

"I mean, I can't promise you'll get the job, but as long as you don't go into the interview wearing a bikini, I think you've got it sewn up."

"You mean I can't even wear my special job interview bikini?" Here she'd been, worrying about Meredith showing up when all Meredith had wanted was to apologize and make something good happen for her. "Listen, I really appreciate your doing this for me. I never thought I'd be in the position to say this to you, but thank you."

"No need to thank me. I had a lot to make up for, didn't I?"

"Well…yeah."

"I want you to be happier than you have been, Chrys. Happier in your professional life and happier in your personal life. I'd like you to give me the chance to make you happy there, too."

"I'm sorry—happy where?" Chrys had been daydreaming about the books she'd choose for the international novel class.

Meredith's gaze was intense. "I'm asking you to give me another chance. To give us another chance. I won't fuck it up this time, I promise."

Chrys felt like she had been speeding along in a car which had come to a harsh, brake-squealing stop. "Wait a minute. You found a job for me so I'll take you back?"

"No, no, it wasn't like that." Meredith held up her hands like a traffic cop telling an oncoming vehicle to stop. "I got you the job because you deserve it. It wasn't so you'd feel obligated in any way to take me back."

"Well, that's good to know because I've met someone else."

"What? Here?" Meredith looked around as if expecting lesbians to emerge from the woods.

"I know it's not exactly a gay mecca. Falling in love was the last thing I expected when I came here, but it happened."

"You're not related to her, are you?" It was the tone that Chrys had always found annoying even when she and Meredith were together—the clipped tone of snarkiness borne out of privilege, the tone that meant Meredith was rapidly descending into a sulk.

"You know I never thought those kinds of jokes were funny." Not from Meredith anyway, who wasn't Appalachian and therefore had no right to tell them.

As Chrys looked at Meredith, she also saw the years that she and Meredith had spent together. There had been lots of good times, no doubt. But had the good times been because of Meredith herself or because of the luxuries and excitement that Meredith's money and status could buy? Money and status were such integral parts of Meredith's personality that, if she were stripped of them, who would she be?

Suddenly, Chrys's time with Meredith felt not like her real life but like an extended vacation, a six-year luxury cruise. For a while it had been great, being pampered and indulged, wallowing in the luxuries that had never been a part of day-to-day life. But when a cruise goes on too long, you start to get sick of the fruity cocktails and the midnight buffets and the hours of basking on the deck, and the boat, no matter how gorgeous, feels like a prison. You realize that it's been a long time since you've done anything worthwhile. It's time to go home.

"Listen," Chrys said. "The job sounds great. It really does. But when I get another job, I want it to be on my own merits and not because someone bought it as a gift for me." She stood up. "The way I see it, you apologized, and I forgave you. Now we don't owe one another anything." She walked into the house and closed the door behind her.

"Now that was something," Nanny said. She was literally on the edge of her seat in her recliner.

"Nanny, did you eavesdrop on me?" Chrys crossed her arms but smiled to show she wasn't really mad.

"I did. I put *Wheel of Fortune* on mute and listened to every word. I know it was wrong, but you know what? They've done took about all the soap operas off the TV. I've gotta get my stories from somewhere. So that doctor you brung up here that time was your…lady friend?"

"She was before she dumped me for a girl half her age."

"Well, I never liked her nohow," Nanny said. "She put on airs. And you can bet if you took that job, she'd never let you forget who got it for you."

"I know it." Chrys took a deep breath, and it felt like all the fresh air in the world was filling up her lungs. "Hey, do you want a bowl of ice cream? I want a bowl of ice cream."

Nanny grinned. "I've done been naughty once today. I might as well be naughty twice. I reckon the Lord will forgive me."

As they sat in the living room with their ice cream, Nanny said, "Did you tell her a fib?"

Chrys licked her spoon. "Tell who a fib?"

"The doctor lady. Did you tell her a fib when you said you'd done met somebody else?"

Chrys sighed. It was impossible to keep anything from Nanny. "No, it was true."

Nanny was back on the edge of her seat. "Well, who is it?"

Chrys almost didn't want to say anything—the day had already had an exhausting amount of drama. But now that she and Nanny had their unofficial policy of honesty, she had no choice. "It's somebody you know."

"Oh, you're gonna make me guess, are you?" Nanny ate a spoonful of ice cream, looking thoughtful. "Is it Dee?"

Chrys feared she might be blushing. "How did you guess?"

Nanny rolled her eyes. "Lands sake, child, who else could it be? She's the only girl you've met around here except for some old biddies at church. I didn't have to be no Jessica Fletcher to figure it out."

Chrys smiled at the reference to *Murder, She Wrote*, a show Nanny had watched addictively when it was on the air. "No, you didn't."

Nanny's face turned thoughtful again. "But Dee's been married and she's got that little girl. I didn't figure her for being...like you."

"I don't think she did either until recently. It happens that way sometimes, that it's just a matter of meeting the right person." Chrys hoped fervently that she was the right person for Dee.

"I reckon that's how it was with your aunt Hazel," Nanny said, setting down her empty ice cream bowl. "But you know, her friend took real good care of her when she was sick and was right there with her when she died. I know the people

I go to church with would say the way they lived is against the Bible, but what about Ruth and Naomi? They was in the Bible, and it seems like they could've been that way."

"It does. Jonathan and David, too."

"That's right. I hadn't thought of them," Nanny said. "I tell you, you sure got me studying on some things I wouldn't have thought about if you hadn't come here this summer."

"I think I could say the same to you."

Nanny laughed. "Shoot, if we spend much more time together, we'll both be so smart nobody'll be able to stand us."

* * *

Anna had painted a banner that was stretched across Chrys's parents' porch: *GOOD LUCK, AMBER, DUSTIN, PEYTON AND CHRYS!* The last family cookout of the summer was doubling as a sendoff, and Chrys's mom was dabbing at her eyes as they all sat around the picnic table. "You remember them Disney nature programs and how I used to cry when the baby birds flew out of the nest?" she said, sniffling.

"I do, Mommy," Dustin said, taking a swig of PBR, "but I'm thirty-eight years old. If I was a bird you'd have kicked me out of the nest a long time ago."

"If you was a bird, you'd have been dead of old age a long time ago," Amber said.

"If I was a bird, I'd be princess of all the birds," Peyton said, flapping her arms.

"You would, honey," Chrys's mom said, gathering her granddaughter in for a hug, then turning to Chrys. "And I know you was just kinda visiting the old nest, but I sure got awful used to having you around."

"Well, I have plenty of good reasons to come back often," Chrys said and looked over at the good reason who was sitting next to her.

Dee looked back at her and smiled. "We're going to take turns on the weekends, one weekend in Knoxville, then one weekend here. It'll be good for Anna to spend a couple of weekends a month in the city."

"And it'll be good for me to be able to look in on Nanny and make sure this so-called caretaker of hers is really doing her job." Chrys had been teasing Nanny about the certified nursing assistant who would now be staying with her, but in all seriousness, she had been impressed with the woman, who was not a pill-stealing twenty-year-old but a fifty-year-old mother of two grown children. She seemed to genuinely enjoy looking after Nanny and listening to her stories while she worked on her crocheting.

"Well, I already know she's a better cook than you. Not that that's saying much," Nanny said.

"I'm trying to teach her," Dee said, laughing.

"Well, I wish you luck," Nanny said.

Chrys held Dee's hand and looked at the faces that surrounded her. She was a little sad to be leaving, but she knew that though she could be a frequent visitor, she couldn't stay. She had classes to teach, a new book to write, and—she squeezed Dee's hand—the gift of a new relationship to unwrap. She didn't know for sure where any of this was going, but that was okay. The faces surrounding her told her where she came from, let her know she wasn't alone, and gave her hope that she might be heading in the right direction. That was enough.

Bella Books, Inc.

Women. Books. Even Better Together.

P.O. Box 10543
Tallahassee, FL 32302

Phone: 800-729-4992
www.bellabooks.com